The Stone of Integrity

BOOK THREE OF THE CENTAUR

CHRONICLES

M.J. Evans

Dancing Horse Press

Foxfield, Colorado

Copyright © 2018 by M.J. Evans

M.J. Evans/Dancing Horse Press

7013 S. Telluride St.

Foxfield, Colorado

www.dancinghorsepress.com

Book Layout ©2017 BookDesignTemplates.com

Ordering Information:

Quantity sales. Special discounts are available on quantity purchases by corporations, associations, and others. For details, contact the "Special Sales Department" at the address above.

The Stone of Integrity/ M.J. Evans —1st ed.

ISBN 978-0-9966617-8-2

Contents

Award-winning author, M.J. Evans loves her Savior, her family, her friends, her horses and poodle, and writing...in that order. A life-long equestrian, she enjoys competing in dressage and exploring the

This book is dedicated to everyone who chooses to live their life with integrity.

"Stand therefore,

having your loins girt about with truth,

and having on the

breastplate of righteousness.

Eph 6:14 (KJV)

CRYSTONIA
NORTHERN REACHES
SWIRLING SEA
LAND BEYOND
MT. HEILODIUS
FT. HEILODIUS
LAKE MANTLE
BY-BASILIA
MT. DASHMORE
MADIERA
FOREST OF RUMORS
RAINSHEEN
CLIFFS OF CONFUSION
HILLS OF HENESEE
D. ENTON
MANION CANYON
ECHOING PLAINS
N
LAND BEYOND

CHAPTER 1

The Map of Crystonia

CARLING REACHED UP AS high as she could and rapped her delicate knuckles on the rough wooden door. She shuffled her feet with impatience, put out that her journey home to her village of Duenton was being delayed. But when Adivino, the historian of the Minsheen herd of Centaurs, summoned her, she knew it must be for a good reason and required her immediate attention.

The door swung open. She lifted her chin and looked into the face of the historian as he greeted her with a warm smile. "Come in, my dear," Adivino said as he motioned for her to enter his cottage.

Carling stepped directly into the old Centaur's sitting room. It felt crowded by time and dust. The wooden plank bookshelves that lined the walls sagged under the weight of hundreds of scrolls, the history of an entire race squeezed into a single room. A large, intricately carved desk set in front of a formidable fireplace formed the focal point of the room. The surface of the desk was piled high with more scrolls, quill pens and bottles of ink in many colors.

"You wanted to speak with me?" asked Carling, walking across the room and stopping in front of the desk. The young Duende's three-and-a-half-foot height enabled her chin to just barely reached the top of the desk.

"Yes, my dear," said Adivino, as he stepped around the desk and turned to face her. The old Centaur shuffled his four legs stiffly due to his advanced age, but his eyes sparkled with the sharpness and intelligence of youth. He looked down at the tiny Duende with her fairy features and startling violet eyes.

Carling didn't quite know how to interpret the look on his face. Was it sympathy? Compassion? Maybe concern? She didn't know. She waited for Adivino to explain his summons.

Adivino smiled again but this time Carling noticed that his smile seemed forced. She pressed her lips tightly together and took a deep breath. The old Centaur always took such a long time to say anything. Carling struggled to push away the irritation she felt building inside her. She was eager to get home and wanted to be on her way to her village by now. As she continued to wait, she bit her lip and twisted her hands together but said nothing.

After several minutes passed slowly by, Adivino spoke. "I have something I want to give you." He shuffled through the pile of rolled-up scrolls on his desk until he found the one he was looking for. To Carling, they all looked alike, but Adivino seemed to recognize each one as well as a hen recognizes her chicks.

Adivino pushed aside quills and ink to clear a place on the top of his desk and unrolled the scroll. Carling gasped when she saw what it contained. Spread out before her was the map of Crystonia she had seen for the first time in this very cottage several months earlier. Adivino had shown it to her when she came to get the historian's help with finding the Stone of Courage. The old Centaur used the map to show her where the Northern Reaches was located. She didn't have time to study it carefully at that point, to get a really good picture of this Kingdom she must rule someday. But from her brief study of the map, she realized how enormous her kingdom was and how many different regions there were. It frightened her to realize how much she had to learn about the vast land of Crystonia. Now Adivino was offering this beautiful map to her.

"Carling," Adivino said, "as the future Queen of Crystonia, you should have this map. It was given to me by Jayceph, the Centaur Historian who preceded me. It is very old, so old that Jayceph didn't even know its source. It is imperative that you keep careful track of it at all times, as this is the only one in existence. If something should happen to it, we would not have a map of the kingdom." He ran his fingers through his hair and added, "I've been meaning to make a copy of it, but," and he made a sweeping motion with his arms, "as you can see by all this mess, just keeping the Centaur records has filled every minute of my time."

The impatience and irritation that Carling harbored dissolved like sugar in water and she was filled, instead, with gratitude. "Oh, Adivino, I am truly honored that you would entrust this map to me. I promise to take good care of it."

"See that you do, my dear," Adivino said. "See that you do."

CHAPTER 2

Zarius

IN THE ROUGH AND ramshackle fort built on the slopes of Mount Heilodius, a herd of rebellious Centaurs made their home. Having split off from the Minsheen herd of Centaurs, the rebels were determined to capture the throne and rule the kingdom of Crystonia...not wait for some prophesied wearer of the Silver Breastplate to appear and claim the seat of authority that had remained vacant for so long.

Zarius, a former leader of the Minsheen herd, took control of the Heilodius rebels through a vile and treasonous act. Now, he wore the shirt of the Commander. Healed, at last, of the injury, but not of the shame, inflicted upon him by Carling when last their paths and swords crossed, he paced back and forth in his quarters in Fort Heilodius. The desire for power ached within Zarius, and he found it impossible to contain or conceal. Yet, here at the fort, as opposed to in the City of Minsheen where he once served on the ruling council, he was surrounded by like-minded Centaurs. As the new Commander, he realized how important it was to keep others in control with an iron hoof. He directed their energies and ambitions with constant drills and long hours of training, sleep deprivation and mental manipulation.

The Commander stopped pacing and kicked the gong hanging by his desk. The horseshoe nailed to his hoof connected with the brass in a loud, irritating BONG! The doors to his chamber burst open and a young Centaur colt, much smaller in size than Zarius, entered the room. "You bonged?" he said with a deep bow of his head and chest from his human-like upper body.

"Gather my generals. I wish to meet with them immediately."

"It shall be done Your Eminence." The colt swished his tail and backed out of the room, closing the doors in front of him.

Zarius approached the large mirror hanging on an otherwise empty wall. Lifting his chin, he examined himself. *Impressive!* he thought as he ran his fingers through his long, dark hair and smoothed his black and silver shirt over his chest. His black horse body shone with health and vitality. His hooves were long but perfectly trimmed and polished. He glanced down at his arm. Even the injury inflicted upon him during his embarrassing confrontation with Carling, was well healed, leaving not a scar. *The Minsheen Herd may have rejected me as their leader but the Heilodius recognize my true talents and abilities...of course, I didn't give them a choice,* he thought. A sinister chuckle escaped his throat. *It is time to address my followers and put them to work.* The Centaur whirled on his haunches and left the room.

When Zarius reached the large but unattractive room built to house the leaders of the Heilodius Centaur army, the generals were already gathered, talking in small groups or milling around with impatience. When Zarius entered, all became silent. All eyes focused on the Commander.

Without making eye contact with any of them, Zarius marched up to the front of the room, his hooves pounding out a four-beat rhythm on the uneven wooden planks on the floor. Slowly, deliberately, he turned to face his followers.

"I have called you here because I sense a change in the air." He paused and looked over the generals. He took a deep breath, expanding his chest. "The Duende girl, Carling, is becoming too powerful. If we do not step in, she will gather the third stone for that silly breastplate she wears. With each stone, the races of Crystonia become more aware of the Silver Breastplate and more convinced that she is the rightful heir to the throne. We cannot allow this to continue. As meaningless as the Silver Breastplate is, there are far too many who are gullible enough to believe in its authenticity."

At this, a few of the Centaurs looked at one another. They were present when a beam of light from the Silver Breastplate worn by the Duende girl struck one of their own and killed him. These few were not convinced that it was a meaningless artifact, regardless of what Zarius was saying. Yet, even they remained committed to the

Heilodius cause...to secure the throne and rule Crystonia.

Zarius continued, his voice gaining in volume with each word. He pawed the floor and, on occasion, reared up on his hind legs. "We must stop her now! I want you to send out your troops. Go to the north, to the Northern Reaches. Go to the south to the Forest of Rumors and the Echoing Plains. Go the east to the shores of the Swirling Sea. Go wherever you need to go to find her...find her and bring her here." Worked into a frenzy, he threw a fist in the air and the Generals followed. With fists shaking over their heads, the Heilodius Centaurs roared their approval, whirled around and cantered out of the room.

CHAPTER 3

Dash for Home

WITH THE MAP SAFELY tucked in her pack, Carling met up with her companions, her best friend Higson, who was also a Duende, and two Centaurs, Tibbals and Tandum. Since the day Carling received the Silver Breastplate from the Wizard of Crystonia, these three had become her constant companions and helpers. Together, they set off toward the village of Duenton, Carling and Higson's home.

The two Centaurs, Tibbals and Tandum, walked at a leisurely pace, winding their way through the trees on the edge of the Forest of Rumors. Their hooves made crunching sounds as they stepped on the red maple leaves that blanketed the ground, signaling the arrival of autumn. Their tails flicked at the nasty flies biting their legs and haunches.

Carling, who was riding Tibbals, let her body move in rhythm with the filly. She was quite an accomplished Centaur rider, having practiced much over the last year and a half that Tibbals served as her primary method of transportation. As she rode through the painted forest, the young Duende, a descendent of the fairies that were once so common across the land, paid little attention to anything but the beauty around her. The red maples intermingled with the thick evergreen pines and firs. Golden aspen shot up into the sky like flaming arrows.

Moving along the edge of the Forest of Rumors was not as intimidating as riding through it, a lesson learned from their journey to find the Stone of Mercy. Along the edge, the trees were not as thick nor as threatening. The light in the meadow was warm and welcoming, the sounds friendly. She was glad of that. The young Duende breathed in deeply the crisp autumn air and sighed as she let out her breath.

"Are you okay?" asked Tibbals, turning her head to look back at Carling.

"I'm just perfect," said Carling with a smile giving Tibbals's long blond hair a playful tug. "Isn't it a beautiful day?"

"That it is, my friend. That it is."

But their beautiful day was about to change.

The two Centaurs, Tandum with Higson on his back and Tibbals carrying Carling, stepped through a chilly, bubbling stream. As he reached the other side, Tandum stopped, cocked his head and turned to one side, his hooves sinking into the mud. The friendly chatter going on between Carling, Higson and Tibbals stopped as well. "Sh-h-h," Tandum whispered, pressing his finger to his lips. "Did anyone hear that?"

Tibbals stopped beside her brother and all four strained their ears to hear. With effort, Carling heard something over the gurgling of the stream. At first it sounded like the rhythmic pounding of a bass drum. Carling's breath caught in her throat...not drumbeats... hoofbeats. And not the three-beat pattern of a canter but the four-beat pounding of an all-out gallop. And it was getting louder!

Tibbals looked at Tandum her eyes wide with alarm. "Centaurs are coming."

"The Heilodius," Tandum exclaimed. "It has to be. Let's move. Higson, hold on tight."

The two Centaurs, with their riders, spun in the direction they needed to travel to reach the village of Duenton. They could no longer afford to enjoy a leisurely journey back to Carling and Higson's home. Now they must run for their lives. Their hooves lifted through the air as though they had wings. So fast were they galloping, it took all Carling's strength to hold on. Her heart beat in rhythm with Tibbals's pounding hooves on the well-packed earth. The wind whistled in her ears and blew Tibbals's hair, which slapped at the young Duende's face.

No one spoke as they ran. They all knew why they were being pursued. Somehow, Zarius, the new leader of the rebel herd of Centaurs knew that Carling was outside the walls of the city of Minsheen. Determined as he was to prevent her from completing the Silver Breastplate and becoming the rightful heir to the throne and ruler of Crystonia, he must have sent his soldiers to find them. It certainly was they who were chasing her. Carling could only guess what they would do if they caught her, and none of her guesses were good. Their only hope was to reach the safety of Duenton before the Heilodius Centaurs and secure the village gates. Yet, even at a full gallop, the village was a couple of hours away, with a steep hogback in front of them that would have to be scaled.

The pounding of hooves and the sound of bodies crashing through the trees and undergrowth continued to grow louder. Tibbals and Tandum were galloping as fast as they could, trying to stay along the edge of the forest for better footing and a clearer path. They panted, and sweat formed on their chests and flanks. But even with their great speed, they weren't going fast enough.

Carling sensed their pursuers were gaining on them. "Higson, get your bow and arrows ready," she shouted, reaching behind her and releasing the bow that was tied to her pack. Holding tightly to Tibbals's belt, she pulled her knees up under her. Balancing like a trick rider in a circus, she pivoted around and plopped back down on Tibbals's back, facing the filly's tail. While facing backward, she reached over her shoulder, pulled an arrow from her quiver and nocked it on the bow string. Her legs tightly wrapped around Tibbals's golden body, Carling pointed the arrow directly behind them.

Higson glanced to the side and saw how Carling was now riding. He raised his eyebrows and shook his head. But, without complaint, turned himself around as well.

Carling watched and waited for the Centaurs to appear while trying to steady herself on Tibbals's back as the Centaur leaped and bounded over the grassy plain.

A Centaur, clothed in the black and silver shirt of the Heilodius herd, burst through the trees that lined the meadow. He was soon followed by several others.

"I see them," Carling shouted. "They're catching up."

"Hold on. I can see the hogback just ahead," Tandum gasped, struggling for air.

The hogback was the steep ridge that bordered the west side of the valley that sheltered Carling's village of Duenton. All four travelers knew the trails well. Carling hoped the Heilodius did not.

Tibbals and Tandum began climbing. The trail carved its way back and forth as it scaled the side of the steep ridge. Gnarled trees and scrub oak lined the path, helping to hold rocks and boulders in place. The footing on the trail was much rockier than the grassy plains and hurt the soles of the Centaurs' hooves. But they ignored this and kept galloping, scrambling up the hillside.

Carling and Higson kept their arrows at the ready, waiting until their pursuers were within range. Both Duende were skilled archers, but shooting from the back of a galloping Centaur while facing backward is a challenge to even the most capable archer and Centaur rider. In addition, there was a limit to how far their arrows would travel accurately.

After nigh on an hour of climbing, Tibbals and Tandum reached the crest of the hogback. Carling looked back briefly and saw the Heilodius halfway up the trail. The Minsheen Centaurs plunged down the east side of the hogback, their eyes locked on the trail, and even then, often stumbling, sending loose rocks cascading down the ridge. Going down was much more treacherous than going up. The steep descent forced Carling and Higson to turn back around and slide forward on the Centaurs' backs until they were pressed up against Tibbals's and Tandum's human-like torsos. The Duende gripped their knees and calves tightly around the horse-like bodies and tried to balance themselves. They couldn't risk falling off and having the Heilodius Centaurs catch up to them.

Halfway down the steep ridge, Carling glanced back. The band of Heilodius Centaurs had reached the top of the hogback and was starting down. "Hurry, Tibbals. They're on the way down."

Tibbals squealed. "I can't go any faster. I'll fall if I do," she said as tears cascaded down her cheeks.

Stumbling and struggling over the loose rocks on the pathway, they reached the bottom of the hogback. Duenton was in sight, just across a wide, grassy, meadow. But the Heilodius continued to close the gap between them. Carling and Higson both turned and released an arrow. Carling's missed its mark, but Higson's struck the arm of the Centaur in the lead. The Centaur cried out in pain and blood quickly soaked the sleeve of his black shirt, but he kept coming. Each of the two Duende reached into their quivers and grabbed another arrow, nocked it, and released. This time, Carling did much better. Her arrow struck the shoulder of one of the band just as he reached the bottom of the hogback. He veered to one side and stopped to snap the arrow in half, leaving the point embedded in his shoulder. With a grimace, he threw the end of the arrow to the ground and crushed it with one of his front hooves. He pressed one hand against the wound to stop the bleeding as the other Centaurs passed him by without so much as a word of concern.

Running as fast as they could, faster even than they'd ever run before, Tibbals and Tandum approached the gates of the village of Duenton.

"Guards," yelled Carling. "Start shutting the gates!"

The Fauns who were on duty in the two watchtowers standing on either side of the gates to the village watched Tibbals and Tandum approach at breakneck speed with the Heilodius Centaurs close behind. They knew immediately that Carling and her friends were in grave danger.

"Get ready to shut the gates," the Fauns in the watchtowers yelled to the Fauns below.

Pik, Carling's friend, recognized her voice. "We can't shut the gates 'til Carling and Higson be safe inside."

"Shut the gates. Now!" yelled Carling from Tibbals's back as they continued galloping forward.

"She said to shut the gates," shouted the Fauns in the guard towers.

"No! Not yet," yelled Pik. "We can't leave 'em outside ta die."

"Shut the gates. Shut the gates," yelled Carling as she grabbed another arrow, turned back and released it. Higson shot two more arrows.

Several Fauns lined up behind the heavy wooden gates. Tensing their muscles, they started to push. With loud scraping noises from the heavy wood planks dragging over the stone surface of the village courtyard, the gates started to close.

Tibbals squealed in fear and lowered her torso to try to move faster. Tandum ran stride for stride beside her, his eyes locked on the closing gates as the opening got narrower and narrower.

"We can't make it," gasped Tibbals.

"Keep going," shouted Tandum as he slowed up just enough to let Tibbals get ahead of him.

Giving up on trying to stop the Heilodius Centaurs with her arrows, Carling spun around and looked toward the closing gates. She felt Tibbals's muscles quiver with exhaustion, her pace getting slower and choppier. "We can make it, Tibbals. Just keep going!" She lowered her body against Tibbals's back, squeezed her eyes shut, and prayed.

The Fauns in the watch towers released a barrage of arrows toward the Heilodius Centaurs. They whizzed over Carling's head just as Tibbals dashed between the rapidly closing doors. Right on her heels, Tandum squeezed through as well, brushing Higson's pant legs on the rough wood. The heavy plank doors slammed shut behind them.

CHAPTER 4

Safe at Home...
For a Time

TIBBALS CRUMPLED OVER AND collapsed on the ground. As nimble as a cat, Carling leaped from her back, thus preventing her dainty foot and leg from getting crushed under Tibbals's heavy horse body. She dropped to her knees beside Tibbals and threw her arms around the Centaur's body. She could hear Tibbals gasping for breath and felt her friend's heart pounding beneath her sweat-soaked shirt.

Higson was soon kneeling beside them. He was not alone. In addition to Tandum, Carling noticed two cloven hooves standing beside her. She looked up and gazed into the small, round eyes of Pikins. The Faun was bending over her, his floppy ears and red forelock hanging down, shading his face. A plaited red beard hung down from his chin. Stuck in one of his two curving horns that adorned the side of his head was a black arrow.

"Pik," cried Carling, "are you alright?"

"What? Me? Oh, this!" The Faun reached up and pulled the arrow out of his horn. "Tis just a scratch it tis. But you should see how many arrows there be stuck in the gates!"

"Are the Heilodius still outside?" Tandum asked.

"Aye," Pik said, "but they not be likin' the welcome we be givin' 'em!" The Faun laughed heartily.

"Are any of the Fauns hurt?" asked Higson, looking up from where he was kneeling beside Carling.

"Nae. We be well protected behind Carling's wall."

"Oh, good," said Carling. "Then I need you to go find Contessa as fast as you can. Tibbals isn't doing well."

A few minutes later, Contessa, the village healer, appeared from the far side of the village square. She carried a jar filled with a pink liquid and was trying desperately not to spill the liquid as she ran toward them.

Contessa lowered herself to her knees in front of Tibbals. "Drink this my darling," she said as she lifted the jar to the filly's lips.

Without questioning, Tibbals drank.

The change was immediate. Tibbals's eyes opened wide. The color returned to her cheeks. She smiled. "Wow! What was that?"

Contessa giggled. "Oh, just one of my secret potions," she said as she gave Tandum a drink as well. "Actually, I can't take credit for inventing it. I got the recipe from Pernilla Persdotter."

Carling jerked her head around and stared, wide-eyed, at Contessa. "I've heard that name before. Where would I have heard it?"

Contessa shook her head. "I don't know. She is a very talented healer who lives in Madiera."

"That's it," exclaimed Carling. "Chamay, the nurse who took care of my broken leg in the city of Minsheen, told me about her."

"Ah, yes. I have seen Chamay at Pernilla's shop when I was there to buy supplies," responded Contessa.

Carling, putting her thoughts of Pernilla aside, turned her attention back to Tibbals. "How are you feeling, Tibbals?"

"Much better. I don't exactly feel like I could gallop back to Minsheen at the moment, but I am so much better." Turning to Contessa she added, "Thank you so very much, Contessa."

"Now, I want you and your brother to rest here for a few days to get your strength back, and heal those chipped and bruised hooves," said Contessa.

"And with the Heilodius hanging around, we need to be rested and ready for anything," added Tandum. "Zarius must have sent his soldiers after Carling. Now they know she has moved from Minsheen to Duenton. We'll need to keep the gates shut to ensure the safety of the villagers."

Carling could tell by the relief that spread over Tibbals's face that the filly liked the idea of staying right where they were. The young Duende felt the same way, and her entire body slowly relaxed, becoming soft and limp. The worry that was knotted up inside of her melted away and was replaced with a sense of security that comes from being home.

CHAPTER 5

The Wizard Returns

THE DAY AFTER CARLING returned to her village, she awakened to the familiar smell of bread baking. It surrounded her like a warm blanket, and she let out a contented sigh as a smile spread across her face. It was good to be back in her village. The little room over the baker's shop had become home to her after her childhood cottage was burnt to the ground by a band of Heilodius Centaurs. Her parents died in the fire, leaving her alone...alone except for her friends. Parkson, the village baker, and his family took her in. She was grateful for their kindness and generosity.

Carling stretched and rolled her shoulders, trying to work the kinks out. Riding a Centaur at a full gallop for two hours is not easy on one's body. She could only imagine what Tibbals and Tandum were feeling this morning.

Carling took off her nightshirt and put on a clean tunic she found hanging in the carved wooden wardrobe that stood across from her bed. She reached for the Silver Breastplate, her constant companion for the last year and a half, and ran her fingers over the green Stone of Mercy and the red Stone of Courage, noting their sparkling beauty and elegant carving. This morning, they felt cold to the touch. At other times, they felt as hot as if a fire burned within them. A shiver went through her as she thought about the power they possessed. Then her fingers moved to the two empty holes. These awaited the last two Stones of Light. Once the breastplate was complete, she would be worthy to be the Queen of Crystonia.

She set the breastplate down and gazed at the beam of sunlight coming through the little round window, lighting the dancing dust particles. *Queen of Crystonia.* That was a title that, growing up in her little village, she never aspired to hold. But she was not given a choice. This responsibility was thrust upon her when the Wizard of Crystonia gifted her with the Silver Breastplate.   Now, she carried the weight of that knowledge around with her just as she carried the breastplate.

No sooner had she placed the breastplate on her body and covered it with a soft, flowing blouse, than Carling noticed the dust particles in the sunbeam start to twinkle. She stopped what she was doing and stared, her mouth dropping open.

The twinkling particles began swirling until they formed a tall column. When they stopped moving and settled to the floor, the Wizard of Crystonia was standing in front of her.

She sighed with relief. "Hello, Vidente," she said with a smile as she lifted her eyes the length of his tall, slender body. She felt her heart start to pound both in eager anticipation and in dread of what this visit signified.

"Carling," said the Wizard of Crystonia, returning the smile, his eyes twinkling. This time, his beard was long and gray. His beard was always changing color and length. The hood of his cloak was not covering his head, and Carling took note of his thick, wavy hair. Today it was the color of polished silver, matching his beard. His slim face was highlighted by his pale blue eyes, eyes that never changed, unlike his beard, and was lined with wrinkles. She loved and revered this face.

"What have you come to tell me?" asked Carling as her fingers unconsciously traced the outline of the two empty holes in her shield.

"The time has come to gather the third stone."

Carling nodded. "As I suspected." The Wizard had sent her on two quests previously, the first to gather the Stone of Mercy in Manyon Canyon and the second to find the Stone of Courage in the Northern Reaches.

"The third Stone of Light is the mystical purple Stone of Integrity. You must find it and add it to the Silver Breastplate."

"Integrity?" Carling asked as she brushed an auburn curl off her forehead.

The Wizard nodded. "Yes. Integrity. It is one of the most important qualities of a great leader. No, let me rephrase that...it is the *supreme* quality of a great leader." The Wizard walked across the room, scratching his head in thought. Then he stopped and turned back to her. "Let me say it is about being true...true to yourself and your subjects at all times, and in all places...no matter what the cost."

"Is that the same as honesty?" asked Carling, trying to grasp the meaning of this complicated concept.

"Honesty is an important part of it, to be sure. But it also involves *all* the choices you make, *all* your actions. Not just what you say, but what you do, how you treat people, how you, as a queen, behave. Always remember who you are...the future queen of Crystonia...and act accordingly."

The Wizard attempted to sit down on the only chair in the room. He quickly saw that it was too small for him so he promptly stood back up, brushed off his robes and cleared his throat. "Let me tell you a story," he began. "This is an ancient fable that I was told as a child. Now I am passing it on to you. As the story goes, there was once a great king. He grew very old and knew that he must go the way of all of us. But he had not been blessed with children to whom he could confer his kingdom. So, he gathered all the children in his kingdom together and gave each of them a seed. He told them to plant the seed, take care of it, and return in one year and show him what the seed developed into.

"One little boy took the seed home. His mother helped him gather a pot and soil and plant the seed. Each day, he faithfully watered the seed and waited for a sprig to break the surface. But nothing happened. Weeks went by and still nothing. There was no sign of a plant. He heard the other children talking about the grand and glorious plants they were tending and his heart sank. When the year was up, the children were summoned by the king to return to the palace with their pots. The little boy did not want to go as he was too ashamed of his failure. But his mother encouraged him. She told him to take his empty pot and explain to the king how hard he tried to take care of the seed and get it to grow.

"With head bowed in shame, the boy took his pot. He entered the palace and saw all the magnificent flowers, plants, and trees the other children had produced. He placed his pot on the floor in the back of the room and tried to hide behind a column when the king entered the room. The king went from child to child as they held out their beautiful plants for him to examine. He nodded at each one but said nothing. Closer and closer he came to where the boy stood, hiding behind the column. The boy dropped his head and waited for the reprimand that was sure to come.

"Looking down, the boy noticed the fancy shoes the king wore stop in front of him. He dared not look up as the other children gathered around and twittered. But the king reached out and took the boy's hand. The king pulled him past all the other children as they pointed and sneered at him. The boy's face flushed red in shame and his heart pounded in fear as he walked beside his ruler.

"The king continued forward, stopping in the front of the room. Turning to face the children, the king said in a loud voice, 'Behold your new king,' The other children gasped. The king continued, 'One year ago today, I gave each of you a seed. I told you to plant it and water it. But the seeds I gave to you were dead. None of them would grow. All of you, excepting this boy, tried to deceive me by planting a new seed. Only this boy displayed the integrity to do exactly as he was told regardless of the consequences. Only this boy has the integrity to rule our kingdom.'"

The Wizard looked deeply into Carling's violet eyes. "The Stone of Integrity will help you be the Queen that Crystonia needs."

"Where must I go to find the stone?"

"It is on the island called Hy-Basilia." The Wizard stepped away and, in a swirl of twinkling light, disappeared just as he arrived.

The New Quest
Begins

THE WOODEN DOOR CREAKED on its hinges as Carling slowly pushed it open. She peered into the dimly lit room built onto the back side of the village blacksmith shop.

"Higson," she said softly. "Higson, are you awake?"

Carling heard the rustling of stiff blankets.

"I am now."

Carling smiled and stepped into the little room, Higson's home since he abandoned his family's cottage in the forest. All the Duende in and out of the village were now the target of the Heilodius Centaurs. Therefore, the Duende from and around the village had moved within the safety of the high walls that Carling, the villagers, and the Minsheen Centaurs constructed the previous fall.

The young Duende girl shut the door behind her. Higson lit the oil lamp beside his bed. The flame cast a warm glow around the sparsely furnished room. Beneath the tiny window was a small bed piled high with coarse, woolen blankets. The oil lamp sat on the seat of a crooked wooden chair beside the bed. A tattered rug covered only a part of the roughhewn planks that formed the floor. A wooden bench sat against one wall. Higson's few belongings, a pack, some items of clothing, a sword, a bow and a quiver filled with arrows, were stuffed in a corner. Other than that, the room was bare.

Carling sat on the wooden bench across from Higson's bed. "The Wizard has returned," she said.

Higson sat up and ran his fingers through his wavy, brown hair. "I knew he would return soon. However," he said, flashing a bright smile as he joined Carling on the bench, "I was hoping to get a bit more rest before we were sent on another quest."

"Me, too." Carling scooted down the bench until she was sitting right next to Higson. She reached her arms around him and hugged him. He returned the hug and held her there.

Carling happily stayed within the warmth of Higson's arms, savoring the love and companionship she felt with him. As she sat beside him, her mind drifted back a few months, to the time Carling battled Zarius, the new leader of the Heilodius herd of Centaurs. The humiliation the Centaur suffered when Carling bested him in a sword fight showed on the Centaur's face and in his parting words: "We will meet on the field of battle again." The cold, hard, look in his eyes and the bitter, angry words were the stuff that filled Carling's nightmares ever since.

Carling wished she could stay right there...safe in the encircling arms of her friend that she loved so much. She always knew she could count on Higson to help her. She remained sitting on the bench next to him for several minutes, enjoying the feel of Higson's hand as he stroked her hair.

"So, where to this time?" Higson whispered.

"The island called 'Hy-Basilia'," she said softly, not wanting to break the spell of this moment.

With the sun now fully up, Carling and Higson left the room behind Ashtic the blacksmith's shop to find Tibbals and Tandum. They found their two friends in the home of Contessa, the healer. Very few structures in the village of Duenton were large enough to house a Centaur, let alone two of them. Contessa did her best to make her parlor comfortable for two large horse bodies, setting out every blanket and pillow she owned.

Carling and Higson entered the crowded room. As soon as they found a place to sit, Carling told them about the visit from the Wizard of Crystonia. She watched their expressions as she told them of the new quest to find the third Stone of Light, trying to interpret how they felt. It was Tibbals who spoke first.

"Has anyone seen my hoof polish?" Tibbals said as she shuffled through her bag. "I simply can't go on another quest with my hooves looking like this!"

Carling breathed a sigh of relief. Her delightful friend never changed...and she was grateful for that.

Tandum sighed, reached under a little chair and picked up the errant bottle.

"Thank you, big brother," said Tibbals, snatching the polish out of his hand.

"Let me help you put that polish on your hooves," offered Carling.

"Oh, thank you," gushed Tibbals as she held out a front hoof. "I appreciate the way you put up with my vanity without complaint."

Carling dipped the brush into the bottle of paint. She smiled as she thought how endearing Tibbals's vanity was.

Tandum rolled his eyes as he watched his sister. When he spoke, there was a twinge of impatience in his voice. "What do you know about this Isle of Hy-Basilia? I have never heard of it."

Keeping her eyes on Tibbals's hoof as she applied the polish, Carling spoke over her shoulder, "Higson, will you get the map Adivino gave me out of my bag?"

Higson retrieved the parchment scroll that contained the map, and unrolled it across a small table. The extra length of parchment dropped over the edges of the table. Tandum and Higson bent over the aged, fragile map and carefully shifted it around until they found the Swirling Sea and an island off the shore of Crystonia labeled "Hy-Basilia."

"I see it," said Higson enthusiastically. "It's out in the Swirling Sea."

Carling nodded, biting her lower lip as she concentrated on applying the hoof polish evenly.

"It looks like we must go to Madiera and hire a boat to take us there," said Tandum, still studying the map. "I've been told it is a three-day journey just to get to Madiera by traveling on the road that goes around the Hills of Henesee."

"I've heard of Madiera," said Tibbals. "It's a Duende fishing village. That's where the chefs in Minsheen go to get their seafood."

Higson stood up. "Madiera is another Duende village?"

"Yes," said Carling. "I remember my parents talking about Duende they knew who lived there. I guess we'll get to see it for ourselves. Next hoof, please, Tibbals."

"Why must we go *around* the hills?" Higson asked. "It seems from the map that it would be much faster to go right through them."

"It would be if we were able to secure the assistance of a guide," said Tandum. "But the hills are very easy to get lost in and if we got lost we might add several more days to our journey."

While Carling finished painting Tibbals's hooves, the four friends made their plans for their journey. They decided to depart on the morning after next if there was no sign of the marauding Heilodius Centaurs. All four knew the pleasant autumn weather would not last much longer. They wanted to find the Stone of Integrity, add it to the Silver Breastplate that Carling wore, and return before the first snowfall of winter arrived in Crystonia. Once the stone was in its place, Carling would be one step closer to being worthy to be the Queen of Crystonia.

They just completed their plans when Carling heard a knock on the door of Contessa's cottage. She answered the door. On the doorstep stood Pikins with a big smile on his face.

"Pik," Carling squealed. "How good to see you. Come in."

The Faun stepped through the doorway, and squeezed into the already crowded room. His cloven hooves slipped on the smooth surface of Contessa's floor as he walked inside. "I be looking all over the village fer ye."

"Whatever for?" asked Carling. Her heart began beating loudly as she felt panic well up inside of her. "Have the Heilodius...?"

Pik eased her fears. "No, no...nothing bad. I be visited by a friend o' yourn."

"A friend of mine?" said Carling. "Who might that be?"

"The Wizard of Crystonia."

Carling's head jerked back and her eyes widened. "He came to see *you*?" she asked. "What did he want?"

"He wants me to accompany ye on yer next journey."

Carling felt her heart race. *Why would Vidente want Pik to join us?* she wondered.

As though reading her thoughts, Pik said, "He wants me to help ye find your way to Madiera. We Fauns be quite familiar with the Hills o' Henesee. Before we became enslaved by the Cyclops, we loved frolickin' 'round them hills." A dreamy look passed over his face as he looked off into the distance.

Carling pursed her lips as she thought about the day she first met a group of Fauns in Manyon Canyon. They had captured her friends and were on their way to take them to the Cyclops. Pik helped Carling rescue Higson, Tibbals, and Tandum, and Carling won over the hearts of all the Fauns by saving one of them from drowning. Now these Fauns were living in the village of Duenton, charged with protecting the village by guarding the city gates.

Carling took her loyal friend's hand and Pik looked down at her. "We would be honored to have you accompany us," she said with a smile. "You can be the guide we so desperately need."

CHAPTER 7

The Hills of Henesee

AFTER WORKING THEIR WAY through the thick forest that surrounded Duenton, Carling got her first glimpse of the Hills of Henesee up close. During all her childhood ventures hunting with Higson in the forest around Duenton, she had never been near these strange-looking hills. From up close, it was clear that the hills were painted in every color of the rainbow. Some were yellow, others green. But she was surprised to see still more hills colored red, blue, and purple.

Pik skipped along beside them. At the sight of the hills he ran ahead to take the lead. He stopped abruptly in front of the first hill, his arms outstretched. "Aren't they beautiful?" he said, his voice overflowing with excitement. "Have ye ever seen anything like 'em?"

"I must admit they are quite unique," Carling said with a shake of her head.

"Let's go to the top of this hill," Tandum suggested, referring to a purple hill directly in front of them.

"From up there we can get a better idea of the lay of the land."

Pik led the way straight up, and Tibbals and Tandum climbed after him. With their first step upon the base of the hill, a cloud of purple dragonflies burst from the ground, filling the air with the hum of their whirling wings. Covering the ground was a blanket of purple flowers. Carling now understood where the hills got their colors.

The ground beneath the flowers was soft and the Centaurs' hooves sank into the dirt, making the going difficult. Tibbals and Tandum were soon breathing heavily.

"Whose idea was it to climb this hill?" grumbled Tibbals.

"Sorry, Tibbals," said Tandum. "I didn't know it would be like this. Do you want to turn around?"

"No," the filly said, brushing her long blond locks back from her face. "I'll make it."

"Keep comin'! Keep comin'," exclaimed Pik. "Ye will love it up top."

"Is his enthusiasm getting to anyone else?" grumbled Tibbals. Pushing with her hind legs and lifting her front legs, she struggled up the hill.

Carling felt sorry for her and guilty that she was getting to ride. She rubbed Tibbals's back in encouragement while she watched Pik bounce up the hill. *Perhaps his lighter weight is what keeps him from sinking in,* she thought. *Or, perhaps his cloven hooves.*

After much effort, they reached the top of the hill. The sun was high in the cloudless sky. Ahead of them, hills rolled out to the north and the east like mound after mound of rainbow-colored scoops of frozen cream. Carling and Higson slid off the Centaurs.

"Except for their colors, all the hills look alike." Tibbals said, mystified by the unusual landscape. "How will we ever find our way out once we get into the middle of them?"

"Tis why ye need me," said Pik, his chin held high and his chest puffed out. The smile on his face told Carling how pleased he was to be needed.

Tibbals stepped forward and pointed toward two hills in the center. "Let's go right there. I've always liked purple and yellow!"

"Fillies," scoffed Tandum.

"Hey, that's as good a reason as any," she said, lifting her nose in the air and fluffing her golden tresses.

"She has a point there," said Higson.

Carling and Higson climbed onto the Centaurs' backs and they started down the hill, slipping and sliding all the way. Carling continued to be amazed that Pik was able to ascend and descend the hills with little difficulty. *Perhaps Fauns are half mountain goat,* she thought.

When they got to the bottom, they followed Pik's prancing, dancing feet around a red hill, past a green hill, and between an orange and a blue hill. As the sun hung low in the western sky, they reached a valley between a purple hill and one that was covered in yellow flowers and butterflies.

"This is it," said Tibbals in delight. "This is the spot I saw from the top of the first hill."

While Tibbals and Tandum were ready to quit for the day, their energy spent, Pik was more energized than ever, as though the very hills nourished him. He spun around, his arms outstretched, his face aglow. "Oh, tis good to be home again," he said, his eyes sparkling. The Faun flipped himself into back handsprings over and over. "Whe-e-e-e-e-e," he cried in delight as he tumbled up and down the side of the yellow hill.

Carling, Higson, Tandum, and Tibbals watched, smiles stretched across their faces. Soon, all four of them were laughing, caught up in Pik's enthusiasm.

The second day of their journey started out as the previous day had ended: climbing hills or skirting around them. Pik was confident in where he was going so he set a fast pace, always working toward the north, sometimes leading them over a hill, other times around one. Tibbals and Tandum, being well rested, kept up more easily, even as they trotted and cantered through the soft, spongy dirt that covered the hills and valleys.

At last they reached the final hill. They climbed to the top. From this vantage point, they could see what lay ahead. Stretching far to the north was a dry, yellow desert dotted with little clusters of juniper trees. Beyond that, Carling could just make out the gray-blue line that was the sea. The coastline ran to the north and the east as far as she could see. The water extended to the horizon as though it went on forever. Pik told them that a dark spot along the distant shore was the village of Madiera.

They worked their way down the last hill, feeling a renewed sense of energy and enthusiasm. When they reached the bottom of the hill, Carling felt as though they had come to the end of one world and entered an entirely new one. The flowers that covered the Hills of Henesee came to an abrupt stop and the sand began.

Like an endless sea, the desert flowed away into the distance toward the dark line of the shore.

The autumn sun was high above them, turning the desert blindingly white. The energy they felt leaving the Hills of Henesee was quickly drained from their bodies. The Centaurs trudged along, not speaking, keeping their eyes on the faint, dark outline of a village far to the north. Pik became more subdued, having left his childhood playground behind. He walked beside them, head bowed, long ears flopping down the sides of his face.

Carling sat on Tibbals's back, her heart now filled with anxiety. She pondered the story the Wizard told her about the meaning of integrity. A burning in her chest told her this would be one of the most important qualities of a leader. But how to find the Stone of Integrity? The Wizard told her nothing except that it was on the Isle of Hy-Basilia. What was that island like? And would it even be possible for them to get there? She pressed her hands against her head, trying to push out her fears. She wished they would arrive quickly in Madiera so she could get some of these questions answered. Just sitting and thinking can make the time go by awfully slowly and by now, the day seemed to be a hundred hours long.

Madiera

THE SUN SLOWLY, SLOWLY climbed to its height, and then slowly, slowly descended. But by the time it went behind Mount Dashmore, the mountain that sheltered Tibbals's and Tandum's city of Minsheen, just barely visible to the west, the little band of travelers had reached the outskirts of the village of Madiera. Carling was relieved and grateful to be near the end of their journey.

Nestled among rolling sand dunes that bordered the shore was a very old and dilapidated graveyard set on a hill just outside the village. Headstones of various sizes were scattered at odd angles between windblown willows, whose growth was stunted by the harsh conditions, and thimbleberry bushes, getting ready for the winter by showing off their red berries. A movement in the graveyard caught Carling's attention and she shielded her eyes against the setting sun to look more closely. The face of a young Duende girl appeared from behind a crumbling tombstone. Her eyes locked on Carling and flashed with a momentary look of curiosity. Then the young stranger quickly withdrew behind the stone. *Odd place to play,* Carling thought before returning her focus ahead to the village of Madiera.

A cold, wet wind was blowing off the Swirling Sea, bringing with it the taste of salt and the scent of fish. Carling shivered and wrapped her arms around herself, feeling the Silver Breastplate covering her torso.

They entered the village from the south. As they strolled down the narrow streets, Carling noticed how different this Duende village was from her own. The village of Duenton was populated with artisans. Her own mother had been an acclaimed weaver. Others worked with wood, metal, paints, and glass. Thus, the entire village was a work of art. Each shop and cottage, adorned with stained-glass windows and painted shutters, was charming and beautiful.

While the cottages and shops in Madiera were neat and clean, they were far from artistic. Weathered, gray boards covered the outer walls of each building. The windows were small, the roofs steep. The only weaving going on was that of the old fishermen repairing their nets and sails. The art of glassblowing was limited to the gaffers blowing through their blowpipes making round glass floats to attach to the nets. The art of woodworking was being performed by the talented shipbuilders as they built and repaired fishing boats.

The Duende women were busy doing their shopping, scolding their children, and spreading the day's gossip. This, at least, was just like the goings on in Duenton. The thought made Carling smile.

The other significant difference, Carling noticed, was the number of non-Duende roaming the streets. Centaurs and Cyclops mingled with a few Ogres and Fauns as they shopped the fish markets lining the shore of the Swirling Sea. The young Duende's heart began pounding and her breath caught in her throat when she came upon a Cyclops and Ogre walking toward them. She felt Tibbals's body tense as well. The Ogres and Cyclops were vicious, wild opponents. Carling wondered that the races seemed to be getting along with one another in this village. Yet, all throughout the rest of the kingdom, they were fighting over control of the throne atop Mount Heilodius, the throne that was destined to be hers. *Perhaps food is enough of a motivator to get them to cooperate*, she thought. *I'll have to remember that.*

Working their way through the village, they reached the edge of town that bordered the seashore. It was early evening and Carling's eyes were drawn to the sea which was sparkling, the last of the sunlight dancing on its surface. Having never been near it before, she found its vastness overwhelming but exhilarating. The wooden docks that extended into the water were filled with fishing boats which had returned after a long day at sea. The waterfront was a buzz of activity and noise despite the cold, wet winds that continued to blow. As the Duende busily unloaded their catch, the citizens of Crystonia of all races bartered for the best and biggest fish.

Carling noticed Tibbals wrinkle her nose at the strong smell of seaweed and fish. "It smells awful here. I knew there was a reason I don't like fish," the Centaur filly said, rolling her eyes.

Carling and Higson laughed.

Pik looked up at her. "What? How kin ye not like fish, me lady? Tis the gift from the sea, don't ye know."

"Well, that's one gift I think I'll decline," Tibbals said with a swish of her long tail.

"I'd suggest we find a place to bed down," said Tandum.

"Great suggestion," Higson agreed, sliding off Tandum's back. "With all the shoppers that come from outside the village, there must be plenty of enterprising Duende who have built inns. I'll go ask someone."

Higson ran off and disappeared into the crowd of merchants and shoppers. Carling shivered and watched him go, a twinge of concern twisting her heart. But he soon returned. "Follow me," he said with a wave of his arm.

The weary, wind-blown travelers wove their way to the west past the docks. As they walked along, again Carling found she couldn't take her eyes off the sea. With the setting sun, the water turned gray. The powerful waves crashed against the rocks lining the shore, sending sprays of foam high into the air. The wind picked up even more, carrying the sea water with it. Soon, all of them were wet.

Gradually, the street curved away from the shoreline and into the maze of little buildings. A turn to the left brought them to a dead end. In front of them was a surprisingly large building, the same color of gray as all the rest. Over the tall door built into the center of the front was a bright sign, crudely painted with a barn brush, that spelled out the word "INN." No sign ever looked so wonderful to Carling.

Carling slid off Tibbals's back, landing softly on the ground, and walked beside the Centaur as they approached the inn. Tandum opened the door and let them enter first.

Tibbals and Carling stepped into the spacious lobby of the inn. Carling quickly took in the sights of the room using her skills of observation, which had improved since her quest to gather the Stones of Light began. She learned early on such skills would protect her in the dangerous situations she faced. She'd already faced many and would, undoubtedly, face more in the future. Even a setting as seemingly innocent as a rustic inn needed to be examined carefully.

A fire smoldered in the fireplace and gusts of wind frequently found their way down the chimney causing the fire to pop and snarl and sending sparks to float out onto the flagstone hearth. The flame from an oil lamp sitting on an odd-shaped, wooden table, painted the walls with a warm yellow light. A large dining table and chairs sat empty on one side of the room. The blustery wind that howled outside, shook the entire structure, causing the shutters to bang while the wind whistled around the windows and doors. Nature's symphony. However, as old as the building and furnishings were, it was clean and orderly.

An old Duende man sat behind a desk near the rear of the room. He leaned back in his chair and interlaced his fingers behind his head, his round face beaming with sociable delight. His tiny eyes locked on Carling. "What good wind blows you here at this hour?" he said.

"We have come seeking rooms for the night," said Carling. "Are you the keeper of this inn?"

The tiny Duende smiled, rocked forward, pressed his hands on the desk, and stood. "That I am. And if you have come seeking a comfortable room, then you have come to the right place." He looked at all the members of the little group. "I have rooms for Duende, Fauns and Centaurs. I'm sure you will be happy with them." He started down a hallway to the back, motioning with one hand for them to follow. Then he stopped and turned around. "You do have money with which to pay, I presume."

Tandum stepped forward. "Of course, we do."

"Good, good. That is very good," said the innkeeper. Rubbing his hands together in delight, he nodded his head and smiled.

One door at a time was unlocked and opened. "This room is perfect for you, my dear," he said to Tibbals. At the next door, he said, "For you," to Pik. And on down the line until the last room was opened for Carling.

The innkeeper held the door open as his eyes studied Carling. "For what purpose have you come to Madiera?" he asked. The little man raised his eyebrows and waited for her to speak.

Carling wasn't sure what to say. Having never been asked so direct a question, she did not have a ready answer. Sucking in a deep breath, she simply said, "We have come in search of an object that we need."

He cocked his head then nodded. "Well, I wish you luck in your search."

Carling stepped into the little room, shut the door and looked around. The dingy room felt safe enough. That was all she needed for now.

Carling removed the Silver Breastplate and set it in the corner of the room. She draped her cape over it and crawled up onto the four-poster bed. She melted into the soft, goose-down mattress, pulled the coverlet up to her chin, and was soon fast asleep.

Sometime during the night, Carling awoke with a start. The wind whistling around the tall building was causing the shutters outside her window to bang against the outside of the structure. Sure that that was what had awakened her, she rolled over and closed her eyes.

A few minutes later, however, she heard the latch of her door click. She held her breath and listened more closely. The hinges on her door squeaked quietly then stopped. Carling waited, her eyes wide open, staring at the wall beside her bed. Again, she heard a tiny squeak. Carling sat up in bed. In the shadows, she could just make out the outline of a bent-over Duende man...the innkeeper. She was sure of it. He was squeezing his body through the slight opening in the doorway.

"Who goes there?" said Carling, boldly.

The intruder stood upright. "Oh! Pardon me...Pardon me ever so much, miss. I-I-I must have come to the wrong room. G-g-got mixed up in the dark. I'm so sorry," he stammered as he backed out of the room and shut the door.

Carling stared at the closed door, trying to get her heart to calm down. She clutched the quilt tightly around her as she thought about what just happened. *What was he really doing in my room? Could he possibly know about the Silver Breastplate? No. How could he?*

Carling threw back her covers, crawled out of her bed, and tiptoed across the room. Without making a sound, she slid a little chair against the door, hooking the back beneath the doorknob. It took Carling quite a while to fall back asleep.

CHAPTER 9

Pernilla Persdotter

THE NEXT MORNING, THE five travelers gathered in the large lobby of the inn where the table was set for breakfast. The innkeeper invited them to sit down. He avoided looking at Carling. The Duende man served his guests a large breakfast of rolls, cheese, fruits and, of course, fish. He even served carrot juice for the Centaurs. Tibbals pushed the fish around on her plate but didn't eat any. The man said little as he set out the food, still never looking at Carling no matter where in the room he went. Carling noticed this but said nothing and did not mention the event from the night before.

After she was filled, Carling pushed aside the plates, pulled out her map and spread it out on the table. She beckoned the innkeeper over. He hesitated before moving toward her. "Have you ever been to the Isle of Hy-Basilia?" she said as she pointed to its location on the ancient map.

"Hy-Basilia? I have never even heard of it." He pulled a pair of spectacles out of his pocket and settled them on his nose. Bending over, he examined the map more closely. "Where did you get this map? I have never seen a map of Crystonia that included an island out in the Swirling Sea."

Carling pulled the map away and began rolling it up. "It's a very old map," she said. "Perhaps it isn't accurate."

"Perhaps not. Although islands don't just come and go when they feel like it," he said with a chuckle. "I'm just curious, that's all."

"Yes. So are we," said Carling.

"This object you have come in search of...is it on this mysterious island?" asked the innkeeper.

Carling shrugged her shoulders. "We have been told as much."

"Well good luck finding something on an island that doesn't exist," the innkeeper said as he gathered up an armful of plates.

Tibbals, Tandum, Pik, and the two Duende went out the front door of the inn and looked around. The day was much more pleasant than the previous one, warm with just a gentle breeze coming off the water. Carling looked out to the sea. Though a bank of dark gray clouds sat on the horizon, everywhere else, the sky was a cobalt blue.

She turned to her friends. "The only name I know in all of Madiera is that of Pernilla Persdotter. She runs an apothecary somewhere in the village. Let's see if we can find her. Perhaps she knows something about Hy-Basilia and who would take us there."

It wasn't long before they found themselves standing in front of a little, crooked shop. Painted across the thick, glass windows were the words:

Apothecary
Let Pernilla bring you back to health

Carling looked in the windows. She could see a myriad of oddly shaped bottles holding strange bubbling potions. As they opened the door and stepped into the shop, a little bell tinkled above her head. She was immediately overwhelmed by the aroma of drying herbs such as rosemary, basil and clove, as well as garlic, that hung from strings suspended across the ceiling. The walls were lined with jars of more herbs, colorful powders, and strings of teeth and claws. A barrel filled with something orange and slimy stood next to the door. Carling's skin began to tingle. There was magic here. She could feel it. Even the dust in the air seemed to have magic in it.

A voice called to them from the back room. "I'll be right there. Don't let the cat out!"

Carling looked around. Creeping toward the half-open door was the largest, fattest, shaggiest cat Carling had ever seen. She quickly slammed the door shut, causing the cat the let out a long, low growl. It turned, flicked its tail, and leaped up onto a shelf full of bottles, without disturbing even one. It curled up and laid its obese body down, staring at Carling with round, yellow eyes.

A beautiful Duende woman with long purple hair stepped through a curtain that concealed a doorway tucked behind the counter. Her green eyes were large and set far apart. Her rosy cheeks were round, her lips full. She was as short as Higson, average for a Duende. "Well, well, well. What have we here?" she said with a wide, toothy smile.

Carling felt drawn to her immediately. She stepped forward. "Are you Pernilla Persdotter?"

"I am indeed, my dear. And who might you be?"

"I am Carling from the village of Duenton. These are my friends, Higson, Tibbals, Tandum, and Pik."

"My, you certainly have a diverse collection of friends," said Pernilla as she looked from one to the other and back at Carling, still smiling. "Now, tell me dear, to what do I owe the honor of a visit from all of you?"

"Vidente, the Wizard of Crystonia sent us here."

At the sound of the Wizard's name, Pernilla's hand flew to her chest and her mouth dropped open. "The Wizard of Crystonia sent you here? Whatever for?"

"We have come seeking a special stone."

Pernilla looked her over with a shrewd eye. "A stone?"

Carling nodded.

"Can it be? No. It isn't possible." Pernilla walked around to the front of the counter and stopped directly in front of Carling. Lifting her chin and looking at the young Duende with quizzical eyes she said, "Might you be seeking one of the Stones of Light?"

While her friends watched silently, Carling slowly nodded.

Pernilla jumped up and down. "Then it's true! The rumors I've heard are true. The Silver Breastplate has appeared." Suddenly she stopped celebrating. "Wait! The end to the fighting might hurt my business!" She twisted her hair into a bun on the top of her head and fanned her neck. "Oh, what has become of me? How can I be so selfish? There will still be plenty of sick creatures after all."

Pernilla jerked her head and blinked her eyes several times, as though something just occurred to her.

She looked first at Tandum, then Tibbals. "Is one of you the bearer of the Silver Breastplate? Is one of you our future ruler?"

Tibbals and Tandum both smiled, shook their heads and turned to look at Carling.

Pernilla followed their gaze. "You?" she said, her eyes widening. She cocked her head, scratched her purple hair, and waited.

Carling's face flushed and her pointed ears turned red. She swallowed and nodded.

"Well, I must say, I was not expecting one of our own to become the future queen. But I'm delighted. Yes. I'm *very* delighted." She reached over and took Carling's hands. Her eyes were moist and gentle. "You will be a lovely queen to be sure, though I don't envy you the responsibility."

Carling didn't relish the idea herself, but she smiled and said nothing.

Pernilla continued, "But now, on to the matter of the Stones of Light." She let go of Carling's hands. "What more did the Wizard, Vidente, tell you?"

"We are seeking the Stone of Integrity," Carling said. "He said it is on the Isle of Hy-Basilia in the Swirling Sea."

"Hy-Basilia?" she said, twisting her purple hair around a finger. "I have never heard of such a place." She walked around in a circle, scratching her head.

Placing her hands firmly on her hips, she stopped pacing and looked at Carling. "I would suggest that you go down to the docks and talk to an old fisherman named Fyzzle. He has sailed the sea his entire life. If anyone knows of the existence of an island named Hy-Basilia, it will be him."

CHAPTER 10

Fyzzle

WITH TIBBALS AND TANDUM behind her, Carling walked between Higson and Pik. The little group hurried down the hill toward the fishing docks. The day was bright, the sky clear...except for the same gray clouds on the horizon she noticed the previous day. The air carried a crispness, foretelling the imminent arrival of winter. The salty air also carried the scent of fish. Carling watched fishing boats leaving the docks while others, already successful, returned. Fishermen and shoppers representing all the races in Crystonia were milling around the docks, looking for and making deals.

Pik and Carling began inquiring as to where they might find the fisherman named Fyzzle. Most of the locals they asked were too busy unloading their catches to do more than point to the west end of the shore. But a few stopped their work to provide some information.

"Aw, Fyzzle, the old fisherman. He's been around longer than dirt."

"It's Fyzzle ye seek, is it? Be ready for a long, tall tale. I wouldn't believe much he has to say."

"Fyzzle lives in the cabin at the end of the dock, if you can call what he does with his days 'living.'"

"If ye have a question about fishing or the Swirling Sea, Fyzzle is the one to ask. Someone should take the time to write down all his stories. That would serve us well after he's gone," said one wise and compassionate fisherman.

Carling took the lead as they bumped and bounced through the crowds of Duende, Centaurs, Ogres, Cyclops and Fauns. "Excuse me. Pardon me. I'm so sorry," she said as she worked her way between creatures large and small. Higson, Pik, Tibbals, and Tandum moved in her wake.

One Ogre growled at her when she brushed his arm. "Get out of my way you little pipsqueak," he snarled. A Centaur's tail slapped her across the face when she passed. The sting brought tears to her eyes. As she rubbed her eyes, she was pushed against a Faun by a Cyclops. The Faun's arms were full of fish piled so high he didn't see her. All the fish in his arms tumbled to the ground. A large, yellow cat, who had been following them ever since they left Pernilla's shop, rushed forward, snatched the largest fish and disappeared through the crowd, the fish flopping from its maw.

"Oh, no!" moaned Carling as she bent down to help retrieve the fish. "I'm so sorry."

Pik and Higson stepped up to help them. Tibbals and Tandum stood guard by acting as breakwaters in the crowd.

"Can't be helped in a crowd like this," said the Faun. "Don't know that I've ever seen Madiera so busy."

Carling was grateful for his kindness.

As they moved further down the dock, the crowd began to thin, and Carling saw a little cabin at the end of the wharf. A very old Duende man was sitting on a bench in front of the weathered and sagging building, mending a fishing net. Carling knew instinctively that this was the fisherman named Fyzzle. Her pulse quickened with excitement and anticipation as she picked up her pace.

Just as Carling and her friends reached him, the fisherman stopped his work and looked out toward the Swirling Sea. In a slow, dreamy voice, the old man spoke. "The sea fills me with emotion. I love it and hate it equally. And while I have given it my best, it has refused all my attempts to capture it. Whether with words or fetters, it has resisted them all. It has conquered me, but never have I conquered it." He paused and turned his whiskered chin toward her. His eyes were large and pale and covered with a milky film. As he looked toward Carling, his eyes never blinked. "Who has the tide carried to my door?" he asked with a welcoming smile.

Carling felt immediately comfortable with the old man. "I am Carling, a fellow Duende," she said. "I am here with my friends.   We are from the village of Duenton and the City of Minsheen."

"Such a pleasure to be sure," said the fisherman. "And I am known as Fyzzle."

"Yes. We were sent to find you by Pernilla Persdotter," said Carling.

"Aww." He nodded, and the corners of his mouth turned up slightly. "A wonderful and talented healer, that one is. I've found it necessary to take advantage of her skills far too many a time, I'm afraid," he said with a deep sigh. "Speak now. Why did she send you to me?"

"She said you might know about the Isle of Hy-Basilia," said Tandum.

Fyzzle tilted his head back and closed his sightless eyes as if to get a better view of his own thoughts. His mouth twitched and he rubbed his gray whiskers. "Now there is a name I haven't heard for nigh on a hundred years. *Hy-Basilia.* My Granpopi used to tell me stories about it."

"What did he tell you?" asked Tibbals as she folded her long legs under her and settled down on the dock.

Hearing the filly's movements, Fyzzle said, "Yes, make yourselves comfortable and I will tell you a story."

Fyzzle lifted his cap and scratched his balding head as if trying to bring forth memories long buried. When he spoke, his voice sounded far away.

"Just a few hundred years ago, or, perhaps, a few thousand, I do not know for certain as it was long before my time," Fyzzle began with a chuckle, "the land of Crystonia was populated by Fairies and Humans. It was a beautiful place, full of peace and joy. It was rich in resources and all had sufficient for their needs. The Humans and the Fairies lived side by side and cooperated with one another. The Humans were hunters and farmers. The Fairies were craftsmen and artisans. In time, the two races intermarried and the Duende came into being. The Duende were a lovely combination of all that was good in both races, the Fairies and the Humans. They were smaller than the Humans but larger than the Fairies in stature. They were artistic and hard working. They were happy and sociable and got along well with all people. Most of all, they were then as they are now...peace loving.

"All was perfect in the Land of Crystonia until one dark day when a Wizard came into the land. Of course, at first, no one realized it was a dark day. The Wizard swept into the kingdom bringing gifts. He quickly won the hearts of everyone. He convinced the Fairies, Humans, and Duende that he was there to help them... that he would take care of them. They would never have to work again. Their lives would be ideal. Life would be easy with him in control.

"In the beginning, he kept all these grandiose promises. He built playgrounds all around the kingdom where the inhabitants went on holiday. The Fairies enjoyed sunning themselves on the shores of the Swirling Sea. The Humans played in the snow on the slopes of Mount Heilodius. The Duende favored frolicking through the Forest of Rumors. Everything they ever wanted or needed was provided for them. The children loved the Wizard because he closed all the schools, saying he could teach them anything they needed to know.

"He brought in Ogres, Cyclops and Centaurs to do the work that the Crystonians no longer wanted to do for themselves. The first task he sent the Centaurs to do was to build an elegant palace high atop Mount Heilodius...the palace that still stands today. This became the Wizard's home. From there he governed the kingdom and sent out decrees that all were required to obey.

"Initially, the Fairies, Humans and Duende rejoiced in the decrees as they were all directed at the Ogres, Cyclops and Centaurs. These races were directed to work here or work there, do this or do that. But gradually the face of the Wizard changed from benevolent caretaker to malevolent dictator. As though a mask had been removed from his face, the real identity of the Wizard appeared. The citizens of Crystonia learned the hard way that he was not a wizard of integrity.

"His first edict was directed at the Humans. They were no longer allowed to go on a holiday to any of the places frequented by the Fairies and Duende. Then it was the Duende that were restricted from mingling with the Fairies. Vile rumors were spread among the races until the Fairies were suspicious of the Humans and the Humans were afraid of the Duende. Everyone became distrustful of anyone that wasn't of their race. Soon, the races would not even speak to one another."

Here Fyzzle paused and looked toward the sea again, his blind eyes seeing something that only his mind could see. He sighed and rubbed his whiskers as if to give himself the energy, or perhaps the desire, to continue. Carling waited impatiently. She tapped her toe, eager to hear more of the history of Crystonia. She bit her lip to keep from speaking up.

Tibbals did it for her, saying the words Carling wanted to say. "Well, don't stop there. We are all dying to hear what happened."

"Pardon me, dear visitors," Fyzzle said. "It is such a sad story that it expends all my energy just to tell it. Now, where was I?"

"You were at the part where the Fairies, Humans, and Duende were all turning against one another," said Carling.

"Oh, yes." The old fisherman nodded and wiped a tear from his eye.

"Well, as I was saying, because of the Wizard's evil actions, the peace that once filled the land of Crystonia was gone. You see what an evil leader can do. But that was not the worst of it. One dark, cold, winter night, while everyone should have been fast asleep, mobs of Cyclops pounded on all the doors of the cottages occupied by the Humans. The Cyclops went from home to home. If the door was answered, the Cyclops pulled the occupants, who were wearing only their night clothes, out into the snow. If the door was not answered, the Cyclops bashed it down and the Humans in that home were also pulled out into the cold night air. All the Humans were marched for many days until they reached the Land Beyond. No one knows what became of them or where they are now."

"Oh, that is so terrible," Tibbals exclaimed, her hands on her cheeks.

"I didn't know that Humans ever populated Crystonia," said Carling, her brows knitted. She knew very little about Humans. She knew that the Duende were descended from the Fairies but didn't realize that she was also descended from Humans. That race was rarely mentioned in her school lessons. She once read a book about a Human girl who fell in love with a frightful beast and she remembered thinking it was very romantic.

"Of course you didn't, my dear. They were cast out many hundreds of years ago, and with the way they were treated, it's no wonder they never wanted to come back."

"What happened to the Fairies? There are no Fairies in Crystonia now," said Tandum.

"And what happened to our Duende ancestors?" asked Higson.

"The Duende were allowed to stay in the villages of Madiera and Duenton," Fyzzle answered. "And that is where they are now, as you know."

"And the Fairies?" asked Tandum again.

"That is what I am getting to. The Fairies are very wise and intelligent creatures. When they got word of what happened to the Humans, they realized they might very well be next. So, they left the land of Crystonia, every single one of them."

"Where did they go?" asked Carling.

"No one knows for sure. My Granpopi ventured a guess that they are on a magical island in the Swirling Sea...an island by the name of Hy-Basilia."

"Hy-Basilia," whispered Carling as she looked out toward the sea. Turning back to face the old fisherman, she said, "Please tell me, Fyzzle, what became of the evil wizard?"

"Well, as the story goes, there was a great battle between two wizards, one the evil wizard and the other...Vidente."

Carling gasped. "Vidente?"

"Yes, my dear, the very one. Vidente's goodness overpowered the evil one and he was cast out of Crystonia. But not before he vowed to return someday and reclaim his castle and throne."

Carling felt her heart pound. "Has he ever returned?"

"Not yet, as far as I know. Nor do I know if he ever will or if he is even real."

"That is such a sad story," said Tibbals as she wiped a tear from her eye.

"Well, I am merely telling you the story my Granpopi used to tell me. As I say, I don't know if any of it is true or not."

"Fyzzle, I have a very old map given to me by Adivino, the historian of the Minsheen herd," Carling said, pulling the old parchment from her pack.

"Yes," Fyzzle nodded. "I know of the wise Centaur by the name Adivino. He has a reputation of the highest regard. Too bad he isn't a fisherman," Fyzzle added with a chuckle, "then he would be almost perfect."

Carling nodded forgetting that he couldn't see her. "It has the Isle of Hy-Basilia located in the Swirling Sea, off the coast of Crystonia."

"I wish these old eyes would let me look at it," said Fyzzle.

"I'll look at it."

Carling jumped. A young Duende boy, appearing to be her age or thereabouts, stepped around from the side of the old fisherman's cabin.

"Ah-h-h-h, my grandson, Kelfy. I didn't know you were there. Come meet my guests."

Kelfy walked up to Carling. He was tall, nearly as tall as she, and very handsome. Carling sucked in her breath and stared. Judging from his tan skin, bleached blond hair, strong arms and large, calloused hands, he looked as if he spent long hours out in the sun and on the salt water rowing and pulling nets full of fish. But, it was his eyes that captivated her. They bore into her with an intensity she had never felt before.

Higson stepped forward, placing himself in front of Carling, and extended his hand. "Very pleased to meet you, Kelfy. I am Higson from the village of Duenton."

"Pleased, I'm sure," Kelfy said, not taking his eyes off Carling and pausing just long enough to briefly shake Higson's hand. "And who might this be?" he asked, stepping around Higson and smiling at Carling.

Higson pushed his body between them again. "This is Carling, also from my village."

Kelfy cleared his throat and stepped back. "Well, pardon me for interrupting but I heard you mention a map."

"Yes," said Carling, struggling to find her voice. She blushed. *Yes,* she thought. *Is that really all I can come up with to say?* She took a deep breath. "We are trying to find the Isle of Hy-Basilia. It is here on this map, but no one seems to know if it really exists."

"I know the Swirling Sea as well as any fisherman in Madiera," Kelfy said. "If this isle exists, I will know about it. Let me see the map."

Tibbals and Tandum made room on the dock and Carling carefully unrolled the fragile parchment across the rough wooden planks of the wharf. Kelfy crouched down and examined the map. After a time, he looked out at the sea. Pointing, he said, "According to this map it should be right out there where that bank of clouds is sitting."

"Is there an island there?" asked Tandum.

"I don't know. No one dares to go into that fog bank."

"Why not?" asked Carling.

Fyzzle spoke up. "That is the part of the sea populated by the Adaro."

"Adaro? You mean the race that is half fish-half human, like the Mermaids?" asked Tibbals.

"Yes," Kelfy said. "The Adaro are half human and half fish but they are not anything like the beautiful Mermaids. They are very unfriendly. They will shoot vicious, flying fish at any boat that comes near them. And not just any flying fish. These fish will tear a man to shreds with their long, sharp teeth. We fishermen stay away from there. We sail around the fog to reach our fishing waters."

"So, the Isle of Hy-Basilia could be behind that wall of clouds?" asked Carling.

"Yes, I suppose it *could* be," said Kelfy. He tilted his head to one side and pressed his lips tightly together. Gazing out at the sea again, he said, "But I doubt it. It seems we would have seen it at some point."

"Has the fog ever lifted?" asked Higson.

"Not in my lifetime," said Kelfy.

"Then how would you know?"

"Higson," Carling said with a frown. "That was rather rude. Don't you think?"

"Sorry," said Higson with a touch of irritation evident in his voice. "But if the fog is always there, it seems to me to be very likely that the island might be hidden behind it."

"The boy has a point there," said Fyzzle. "But the fact remains, to sail into the fog, you must get past the Adaro."

CHAPTER 11

Hilgalda the Witch

CARLING AND HER COMPANIONS walked up the hill toward the inn. Her head was down and she stared blankly at the cobblestone street as she shuffled along.

"Hey, why so glum?" asked Tibbals. "Just look at all the information we now have." Tibbals patted Carling's shoulder and fluffed her friend's auburn curls.

Without looking up, Carling merely nodded. "But none of it seems good. And how will we ever get to Hy-Basilia?"

"Psst...Psst."

The five companions stopped and turned toward the sound coming from a dark, narrow alley between two shops. Stepping out of the shadows, as quiet as a ghost, a very small Duende girl motioned to them. Her gaunt face and stringy hair were dirty. Her clothing was much too large for her and hung in rags from her shoulders. Her eyes flitted from one to the other of them before looking out to the street, as if she were hiding from someone.

Carling looked at the child closely. The memory of the little girl watching her from behind the tombstone flashed through her mind and she wondered if it was the same child. Seeing her unkempt condition caused Carling's heart to melt. "What can we do for you?"

"It is I who have come to help you. My mistress sent me to find you and bring you to her. But we must hurry. She is not very patient and will be angry if we are late."

Carling stepped up to the little girl and took her hands. They felt as cold as a corpse. "Who is your mistress?"

The little girl pulled a hand free and motioned with her finger for Carling to bend down. She placed a dirty hand by her mouth and whispered in Carling's pointed ear. "She is called Hilgalda...Hilgalda the Witch."

Carling stood upright. "Hilgalda?"

The little girl jerked back and put her finger to her lips. "Sh-h-h-h." She looked from side to side and whimpered.

"Why are you so frightened?" asked Carling, putting an arm around the little girl.

"Hilgalda doesn't want anyone to know she has sent me to find you."

"Why not?" asked Tandum gruffly.

Carling flashed him a look of rebuff, then turned back to the girl. "You don't need to be afraid. We won't let anyone hurt you."

The little girl looked up at Carling with moist eyes. "I know you mean it when you say that. But you don't know the magic that Hilgalda controls."

"Take us to her, then," said Tibbals. "Would you like to ride on my back?"

The little Duende girl's eyes lit up. "Ride on a Centaur? Could I?"

Tandum bent down, lifted the tiny Duende as easily as if she were a little bird, and set her carefully on Tibbals's back. "Now hold on," he said, patting her bony leg.

Carling looked up. "Show us the way to Hilgalda's home."

At the far eastern edge of Madiera stood a little shack set high on a rocky ledge overhanging the Swirling Sea. The little girl pointed up to the shack.

Carling looked back and forth at her friends. "Up there? Oh, my." She took a deep breath. "Okay, then. Let's go up and see what Hilgalda wants."

Tibbals didn't move. "I don't like the looks of the shack or the trail. It looks rather scary to me. Are you sure we should go up there, Carling?"

"You can stay here. I will go up by myself," said Carling, patting Tibbals on the shoulder.

"You're not going up without me," said Higson.

"Nor without me, Missy," added Pik.

"Alright, alright. We'll all go," said Tibbals with a sigh.

They wound their way up a narrow staircase made of stones, well-worn from years of use but over-grown from years of neglect. At times, the path wove right along the edge of the cliff. Giant waves from the sea crashed against the rocks far, far below, sending spray high into the air. Carling shivered. Was it just the cold, moist air or was she also afraid? She remembered the Wizard of Crystonia, Vidente, telling her that courage did not mean the absence of fear. Courage meant doing the right thing even when you're afraid. The young Duende hoped she was doing the right thing. She placed her hand over the red Stone of Courage where it sat nestled in its place on the lower part of the Silver Breastplate. It felt warm to the touch. Its presence comforted her. She gritted her teeth, refusing to look down at the Swirling Sea, and kept moving up the steep staircase.

When they reached the top, Carling looked ahead and saw the front of the shack as it came into view. It was more dilapidated than she originally thought. It was nothing more than a tiny hovel, even when compared to the little houses in the village. Rising from the center was a smoking chimney. Several shingles were missing from the roof, others lay at odd angles. The shutters on the windows hung loosely from rusted hinges and banged against the side of the cabin as the wind whipped around the shack. She heard the bleating of goats coming from an enclosure to the side of the crumbling structure.

Pik perked up his ears. "My people," he said with a smile.

The front door to the shack stood ajar.

"I'll get off here," said the little Duende girl, a tremble in her voice. Tandum lifted her down and she dashed toward the enclosure that held the goats, disappearing behind the vine-covered walls.

Tibbals watched her go. "What I wouldn't do for the chance to give her a bubble bath and curl her hair."

Carling smiled and nodded. "Let's see why we have been brought here," she said, a slight quiver in her voice. The future queen led the way to the open door.

Inside the shack, also dressed in dirty rags, a very old Duende sat at a spinning wheel, magically spinning strands of her hair into silk. She appeared smaller than most of the Duende, perhaps shriveled with age. The remainder of her thin, white hair was plaited into a long braid that hung down her back. Her bony fingers, the knuckles gnarled with arthritis, managed to handle the yarn with skill. A large yellow cat lolled on a bench by the fireplace, her massive paws hanging over the side. The cat opened one eye and looked at Carling. Carling sucked in her breath. She was sure it was the same cat that had followed them from Pernilla's shop and snatched the fish.

Hilgalda the Witch looked up at Carling with intense, green eyes and smiled, revealing yellowed teeth, many of which were missing. "I have been expecting you," she said in a deep, gravelly voice.

"Yes. You sent your...um...granddaughter to fetch us?" asked Carling.

The witch sniffed. "She is not my granddaughter. She is my servant."

"I see. In any case, perhaps you could be more generous with her and get her some clean clothes."

The witch jerked her head back and stopped spinning. "My, you are a plucky one, aren't you?"

Carling ignored the comment. "Why did you want to see us?"

"I have heard, through my various sources, that you want to go to the Isle of Hy-Basilia. Are you aware of the dangers associated with such a journey?"

Carling nodded. Her companions didn't move, not even to blink. "We have been told that the island doesn't exist," Carling said.

Hilgalda chuckled deep in her throat. "Oh, it exists all right. You just need to know how to find it."

"Can you tell us how to find it?" Carling asked.

"It's quite easy, really, *but* you will need to get past the Adaro first. And only *I* have the key to getting past them."

"Are you willing to help us?" asked Tandum, his arms crossed over his chest and one hoof tapping with impatience. The large yellow cat let out a low growl, leaped off the bench and slowly wound its way around each of Tandum's four legs. Tandum ignored it.

"I might be willing. What can you do for me, my handsome young Centaur?"

"What do you need?" Tandum asked.

"I need more hair to spin into silk. Would you give me the hair from your beautiful, long, tail?"

Tibbals gasped and Tandum twitched his tail as he pursed his lips. A Centaur's tail is his prized possession. "I might be persuaded to do that," he said after a long pause, "*if* I can be convinced that the information you give us will really help us."

"Oh Tandum!" moaned Tibbals. "Your beautiful tail."

Pik jumped in. "Take me beard instead," he said as he unbraided his red beard and ran his fingers through it as if to show off its beauty.

"Hum-m-m, not a bad offer, I must say. But the tail of a Centaur...now that is quite a prize," said the witch, a crooked smile on her face. "Just think of the beautiful things I could weave with the tail of a Centaur."

"Tell me what information you will give in exchange for my tail," said Tandum.

"The tail first," snapped the witch. "Then I will show you how to get past the Adaro."

Carling looked over at Tandum then at his beautiful, long tail. She felt her body go slack, as though she was going to collapse. The very thought of Tandum having to make such a great sacrifice brought tears to her eyes. "Tandum, you don't have to do this."

"What other choice do we have?" he said, his voice filled with determination.

The witch jumped up, a pair of long scissors in her hand. Giggling like a mad woman and snapping the blades of her scissors, she said, "He's right. He's right you know. You don't have any choice if you want to get to Hy-Basilia." The cat meowed and dashed across the room. Giggling wildly, Hilgalda grabbed Tandum's tail and chopped it off just below the bone. Holding the long chestnut-colored hairs over her head she shrieked with delight. "It's mine! It's all mine."

Hilgalda froze in place, the sharp point of a sword pressed against her chest. With eyes narrowed and teeth clenched, Carling snarled, "Now tell us what you know."

The Witch's Secret

HILGALDA IMMEDIATELY BECAME SOMBER. "You needn't get so testy young Duende. I have something to give you. If you get that sword out of my way, I'll get it for you."

Carling lowered the sword but continued glaring at Hilgalda. The witch stepped back and lovingly placed Tandum's tail across the chair by her spinning wheel. With an elegance that belied her age and arthritis, she floated to the far side of the room, her cat watching her every move while it twitched its tail.

The witch stopped in front of a dusty, old trunk. She bent over and lifted the lid, the hinges creating with a scratching sound as metal rubbed against metal. After a few minutes of shuffling through its contents, she straightened. In her hand, she held a tiny, wooden flute. "Here it is," she said, holding up the prize.

Feeling a stab of disappointment mixed with anger, Carling cocked her head. "A flute?"

"Oh, my dear, not just *any* flute. This is a flute whose every note is filled with magic." She placed the instrument against her lips and blew into it. A winsome melody floated across the room.

Crash! Carling jumped and turned around. Pik was sprawled out on the floor.

"Don't worry," Hilgalda said as she stopped playing the flute. "He's just asleep. Fauns always respond like that to my flute; as will the Adaro."

Carling ran over to Pik, just to reassure herself that he was all right. He started snoring loudly. She smiled with relief.

Turning back to face Hilgalda, Carling said, "I have been told that the Adaro are in the waters by the fog. Now, am I to understand that the Adaro guard the Isle of Hy-Basilia?"

"That's right, my dear. They refuse to let anyone pass. They do the Fairies' bidding and the Fairies don't want to be disturbed."

Higson, having been quiet all this time, stepped forward. "Then is the island behind the wall of fog that we see from the shore?"

"Yes. You will see it clearly once you are through the bank of clouds that hides it. But I might suggest that you sail at night, by the light of a full moon. The Adaro will sleep longer if it is nighttime. Oh, and one more thing. Don't take the Faun on your journey. He will be of no use to you if he falls asleep."

Sailing to Hy-Basilia

THE CENTAURS' HOOVES CLATTERED on the stones as they descended the very steps they climbed to reach the witch's hut. Pik wobbled as he walked, still groggy from the sleeping spell. Carling rode on Tibbals and followed Tandum who carried Higson. Every time Carling looked at Tandum's tail, she felt her eyes well up with tears. She knew his tail would grow back eventually, but had no idea how long that might take. She clutched the magic flute tightly in her hand, hoping it would be worth Tandum's sacrifice.

They made their way between the weather-worn buildings of the little fishing village, past tables where Duende were selling the day's catch to Centaurs, Ogres, Cyclops and the occasional Faun. They went straight to the docks where fishermen were cleaning their boats and folding their nets. The fishermen laughed and talked among themselves, clearly pleased with the results of their morning's work and happy to be back at the docks so early in the day.

Carling stepped up to the nearest boat. A fisherman was swabbing his boat's deck, his back to them. "Excuse me," Carling called out from where she sat perched on Tibbals's back. "Excuse me, sir."

The Duende fisherman turned around. He started and his mouth dropped open. "A Duende riding a Centaur," he exclaimed. "Well now I've seen it all. This is something I'll tell my children over the dinner table tonight."

Carling smiled. "I'm not sure they will believe you."

"True that," he said, removing his cap and scratching his head.

Carling slid off Tibbals and stepped up to the fisherman. "We are looking for a fisherman who will take us behind that bank of clouds," she said, pointing to the north.

The fisherman's mouth fell open again. He turned and looked out to sea. Whipping back around, he stammered. "Y-y-you wa-wa-want to g-g-go out there?" Ar-r-r-re ya out of your p-p-puny minds? Nobody, and I mean *nobody*, will take you th-there."

"I will."

All heads jerked around toward the speaker. Carling caught her breath and her heart skipped a beat. Standing at the head of the dock was Kelfy, looking more handsome than ever. Though Higson stepped up beside Carling and draped his arm over her shoulders, her eyes remained on Kelfy.

Kelfy stepped closer. "I said I will take you to the fog to see if the Isle of Hy-Basilia is really there."

"You are so brave," gushed Tibbals.

"You are so crazy," sneered the fisherman.

Kelfy ignored both as he gazed into Carling's violet eyes. "If I can be of service to this young lady, then any risks I take will be worth it."

Back at the inn, the group of travelers, now having increased to six, gathered around a lopsided wooden table. Tibbals and Tandum stood. Carling, Higson, Pik, and now Kelfy, sat on old, wobbly stools. The map was spread out on the table before them.

"Hilgalda suggested we sail at night during a full moon," said Carling. "She said the Adaro would sleep longer if we did."

"I'd sleep longer if we didn't," said Tibbals with a yawn.

Carling smiled up at Tibbals, then turned her attention back to the map. "Kelfy, how long will it take us to reach the fog?"

"If the winds are with us, three or four hours."

"And when will there be a full moon?" asked Higson, sliding over until he was pressed against Carling.

"Um-m-m, let me think," said Kelfy, sliding over from the other side until Carling was wedged between the two of them. "It should be the day after tomorrow."

"What supplies do we need to bring with us?" asked Pik.

"Pik," Carling said, her voice a little hesitant, "I'm afraid Hilgalda said it would be best if you didn't come with us."

"What? What be the reason Missy?"

Carling picked up the flute. "Because of this. It puts you to sleep. Remember?"

Pik's cheeks turned as red as his beard and he pulled his forelock over his eyes. "Oh. I forgot. I guess I wouldn't be much help to ye."

"Oh, Pik, you can still help us," Carling said, feeling an ache in her heart. "We will need you to stay here and keep an eye out. I fear that the Heilodius will learn we are here and come looking for us. They won't know you are with us. You can be our eyes and ears while we're gone." Carling reached across the table and patted her friend's hand.

Tibbals flipped one of Pik's long ears. "And with these ears," she teased, "you shouldn't miss a thing!"

After Kelfy left the inn, Higson sat down next to Carling. "I'm not so sure I trust that Kelfy fellow."

"Oh, don't be silly, Higson. We need someone to help us get to the island and he's willing to do it."

"But why is he doing this? What's his motivation?" he asked with a scowl on his face.

"Maybe he just likes us," Carling said, surprising herself that she felt so defensive of Kelfy even though she barely knew him.

"You mean he likes *you*. You heard what he said at the dock. We all did."

Carling snorted. "I'm sure he just wants an adventure."

"You aren't jealous are you, Higson?" Tibbals teased as she ruffled the Duende's hair.

Higson rolled his eyes. "Me? Jealous? Of a guy who smells like fish?"

During their discussions, the innkeeper busied himself sweeping, dusting and stoking the fire. At times, he walked past their table and glanced at the map. All during their discussion and planning, the innkeeper offered nothing by way of suggestion. He just hung around within ear-shot. While the others paid him no mind, Carling did take notice. The innkeeper's "accidental" appearance in her room during their first night's stay still troubled her a bit, though she opted not to say anything to her friends.

The adventurers spent the next two days gathering supplies, food and water mostly, and they filled their quivers with arrows and sharpened their swords. They wanted to be prepared for whatever they encountered when they reached Hy-Basilia...*if* they arrived there at all. Tandum cautioned them to be equipped for anything. Carling left one bow and a few arrows, along with the map of Crystonia with Pik.

Kelfy borrowed his grandfather's fishing boat which he had captained many times before. While not large, the boat was sturdy and Kelfy felt certain it would carry them safely across the Swirling Sea.

Fyzzle didn't like the idea of his grandson sailing through the fog. He confronted the boy when they were alone. "You're a headstrong boy. I know it will do no good to tell you, 'No.' Once you get an idea in your head, there is no getting it out. I just hope you haven't bitten off more than you can chew by facing the Adaro. Many a skilled sailor has been turned back by the monsters' attacks with the flying fish."

Kelfy patted his grandfather's hand. "Don't worry, Granpopi, we have magic with us."

"It better be powerful magic," the old man said before letting out a sigh and returning to mending the fishing net he held on his lap.

Two days later, with the Silver Breastplate tightly encircling her body and the magic flute tucked in its front, Carling led her companions down the hill toward the dock. The sun set to the west, painting the clouds gold and magenta, while the full moon rose in the east. A few clouds floated out to sea and back in again, but the winds on the surface were gentle, perfect for a nighttime sail out into the Swirling Sea.

By this time in the evening, all the fishermen had returned from the sea, sold as much of their catches as their customers would buy, and brought the rest home to their families. Except for a large rat with round, pink eyes and a long hairless tail scurrying around searching for discarded fins and fish heads, the wharf was silent and empty. Carling, Pik, and Higson arrived at Kelfy's boat first, carrying baskets of food. Pik's cloven hooves made a clicking sound on the rough boards of the pier. Pulled by the moon, the waves splashed against the pilings supporting the dock and rolled over the natural rock jetty protecting the bay.

Kelfy was busy readying the boat when they arrived. He looked up and gave them a warm smile and quickly turned his eyes to Carling. "You made it...at least some of you. Where are the Centaurs?" He extended his hand and helped Carling step down into the rocking hull.

"They're on their way with the water," Higson said as he jumped down and took Carling's baskets of food from her.

Pik lowered the supplies he'd brought into the boat. "Do ye have everything ye need?"

"We will when Tibbals and Tandum get here,"
Carling said. "Are you going to be okay, Pik?" she asked,
her violet eyes reflecting her concern.

Pik waved his hand. "Aww Missy. Don't ye worry
your pretty little head 'bout me. I kin take care o'
meself jess fine. And I'll be on the watch out for the
Heilodius, that I will. Ye kin count on me."

Tibbals and Tandum hurried down the dock, their
hooves clip-clopping loudly on the wooden planks.
Each of their arms held an earthen jug. Tibbals was
frowning and bent over. It was obvious that the jugs
were quite heavy. Kelfy leaped out of the boat and ran
up to Tibbals, with Higson right behind him. Each
Duende relieved Tibbals of her load by wrapping their
arms around a jug. They shuffled their feet under the
weight until they reached the boat.

Tandum stopped and scrutinized the boat. "Will that
thing carry me?"

Kelfy grunted and huffed as he lowered the four
water jugs into the bow, making the boat rock forward.
"Sure, it will. There isn't a more seaworthy ship in all of
Madiera I would venture to say." He pulled a rag from
his back pocket and wiped sweat off his forehead.

Within a few minutes, all who were sailing were in
the boat, their weight causing it to sink low in the
water. Kelfy peered over the side and frowned, then
placed his oar in the rowlock and pushed away from the
dock. "Everyone get comfortable. We have a long
journey ahead to get across the sea. We're mighty low
in the water. That will slow us down."

Getting comfortable was fine for Carling and Higson.
They sat on the center thwart, the wooden bench that
extended from one side of the boat to the other. But for

Tibbals and Tandum, getting comfortable was entirely another issue. Trying to position a large horse body in a boat built for little Duende was not easy. With grunts and groans, they lowered themselves to the burden boards that covered the bottom of the boat and prepared to ride it out.

Carling turned and looked back at Pik. It was too dark to see his expression, but she was sure he was sad. Perhaps it was just that she was sad to be leaving him. All she could see was a little wave of his hand as they sailed farther and farther away. "Good bye, Pik," she shouted while cupping her hands on either side of her mouth.

"Find what you're looking for," he yelled back. His voice floated away on the breeze.

Kelfy was, indeed, a skilled seaman. He hoisted the well-worn sail until it reached the top of the mast and secured it at the base. Then he sat in the stern of the boat and directed the sail by moving the boom to catch the breeze just right. Soon they picked up speed and sailed around the jetty and out into the open sea.

Carling pulled the flute out from beneath the Silver Breastplate, where it had been pressing uncomfortably against her chest. She gripped the gunwale with one hand as she clutched the enchanted flute in the other. The boat rocked gently up and over the rolling waves. She kept her eyes looking due north, toward the bank of clouds that sat on the horizon. The warm, white, winter moon drew a line on the water, leading them straight toward the bank of clouds.

The farther away from the protection of the harbor they sailed, the rougher the seas became. Soon, poor

Higson was hanging over the gunwale, leaving his dinner behind. Carling slid over and rubbed his back. "Oh-h-h-h," he moaned, "I was not cut out to be a seaman. I like my feet on something more solid."

"I couldn't agree more," said Tibbals. "My stomach is complaining violently." But since she was half horse and horses cannot vomit, the filly just had to endure the pain in her stomach.

Kelfy, was, of course, not the least bit affected by the rocking and rolling. With constant little adjustments of the boom and the rudder, he kept the boat on the wiggling white line the moon painted. His eyes remained glued to the north. There was just enough wind to keep them moving swiftly.

After a few hours on the sea, the cloud bank loomed large and close, threatening them like a monster from a nightmare or, as in Tandum's case, a nightstallion. "We're almost there. We should be approaching the home of the Adaro," said Kelfy.

These words just left Kelfy's mouth when several flying fish sailed over their heads, some splashing back into the water but many landing in the boat. These were not ordinary flying fish. The fish sported a mouthful of teeth with which they were known to bite the arms and legs of sailors. They had razer-sharp fins that they used to cut and slice clothing. While some of the fish began slicing holes in the sail of Kelfy's boat, others worked at chewing and cutting the oars and sides of the tiny craft. Kelfy struggled to lower the sail to protect it, and Tandum and Higson each grabbed their swords and began swatting at the fish as they flew through the air.

The sound of laughter reached the ears of the travelers, but it was not the happy sort of laughter one hears when creatures are having fun. This laughter was menacing and filled with evil. All around the little fishing boat, Adaro were rising out of the water, flinging flying fish toward the vessel...and laughing!

Carling held up her arms to shield herself and looked over the side of the boat. When she saw the Adaro lifting halfway out of the water, she gasped and pulled back. Her entire body began to shake uncontrollably. The Adaro were, indeed, monsters. Their heads were shaped like human heads but they were as thin as skeletons. A single fin sprouted in the center of each Adaro's forehead and stretched back over the top of the head until it reached the back of the neck. Their shoulders and chests were clothed in shells and seaweed. Their muscular arms were covered with slimy scales. As they laughed, their pointed tongues waggled between sharp teeth. Their large round eyes glowed with a white light.

Tibbals looked over the side as well and screamed at the sight. She screamed again as a fish became entangled in her long hair. Tandum twisted around until he was on his hooves. He struggled to remain standing as he continued swinging his sword over his head, chopping at the fish. Higson stood as well. Carling and Tibbals ducked their heads to keep away from the swinging swords.

The boat began spinning around. "I can't control it," shouted Kelfy. "I can't control it! Hold on!"

With the attack underway, Carling left her seat and worked her way toward the bow of the boat, dodging Higson's swinging sword. She crawled over Tibbals, who was grabbing at the fish in her hair, and onto the forward thwart. She kneeled on the board and tried to steady herself. The young Duende placed the flute to her mouth just as a fish flew through the air and grabbed hold of her arm with its sharp teeth. She gasped from the pain but sucked in enough air to begin playing the little wooden instrument. The first few notes were weak and shaky, but she kept at it until a mournful melody began floating through the salty air and over the choppy, spinning water.

At first, the music produced no noticeable results. The attack kept coming. The boat kept spinning. The fish kept flying. Then everything changed. The water calmed, and the boat stopped spinning. The fish disappeared. Except for the mournful notes from the flute, everything became deathly, hauntingly, quiet.

The five sailors sat still, looking from one to another. No one said a thing as they all waited to see what might happen next. Carling continued to play her flute, fearful that if she stopped the Adaro would awaken and the battle would begin again. The magical notes floated over the still, black water.

Tibbals gathered the courage to glance over the side of the boat once again. Adaro surrounded the boat, in various positions of repose. All were sleeping soundly, some smiling, others frowning as they visited their dreams.

"Let's get moving," said Tandum, "while we have the chance."

Tandum and Higson sheathed their swords, grabbed oars and dipped them in the water. They were careful not to hit the Adaro. Kelfy raised the sail and adjusted the boom so that the cloth, even with the slashes caused by the flying fish, caught the wind. With the skill born of a life on the Swirling Sea, Kelfy piloted the boat toward the seemingly impenetrable wall of fog.

All felt great relief as they left the sleeping Adaro behind. But the relief was replaced with apprehension when they found themselves completely engulfed by thick, cold, dripping clouds. Carling lowered her flute and silence surrounded them. The young Duende remained in the front of the boat and peered ahead. Nothing. She could see nothing. The water and the fog seemed to melt together and become one.

The silence was broken by a clap of thunder. "A storm is coming," yelled Kelfy. "It will soon be upon us. Hold on."

The boat started rising and falling as the Swirling Sea sent giant swells toward them. Carling and Tibbals clasped the sides of the boat.

They continued to rock up and down through the thick fog. The wind began tearing at the sail. Tandum and Higson pulled at the oars, grunting and panting from the effort.

"Are we going the right way?" shouted Tibbals as she pulled wet strands of long hair away from her face.

"Don't worry. I can handle this," said Kelfy through clenched teeth.

"Can I do anything to help?" shouted Carling over the howling of the wind.

"Just stay seated," said Kelfy as he strained at the boom. "I don't want to lose you."

Carling noticed the set of Kelfy's jaw and the tenseness of his muscles as he pulled and pushed, fighting the wind. She glanced over at Higson and noticed that he was watching her. She managed a weak smile. He said nothing while he struggled to keep rowing.

The darkness evaporated in a flash of lightning. At that very moment, Carling looked over the bow of the boat. Above her was a dark, threatening sky. Before her was the black plane of the sea, its surface boiling and bubbling with the approach of the storm. And ahead of her was the dark outline of an island.

CHAPTER 14

Caught in a Storm

CARLING LEANED FORWARD, CLASPING the bow of the boat with both hands, squinting her eyes to see more clearly. Could it be? Could it possibly be? Yes! Ahead of them was an island, barely visible each time there was a flash of lightning.

Carling's heart pounded against the Silver Breastplate. She began trembling. "I see it! I see the island."

Everyone stopped struggling with the wind and the waves and looked ahead.

Storm clouds blotted out the moon and stars, and smothered the boat and its passengers in thick, dripping darkness. The approaching storm brought gusty winds that sent their boat skimming swiftly across the waves directly toward the dark outline of the island. The occasional flash of lightning that shimmied across the water provided a back-light, and they could just make out the shape of the landmass ahead of them.

It was large, extending so far in both directions that they could hardly see the end of it. In its center, a tall mountain the size of Mount Dashmore, provided the capstone.

The winds became stronger and more violent, sending them faster and faster over the rolling waves. Higson and Tandum pulled in their oars and joined Carling and Tibbals as they gripped tightly to the gunwale. Kelfy abandoned his hold on the boom and rudder. The boat was out of his control. It was as though they were a fish on a line and the island was the fisherman reeling them in.

Carling kept her eyes glued to Hy-Basilia as it loomed larger and larger in front of them. One hand held tightly to the rail. With the other, she tucked the magic flute beneath the Silver Breastplate where it again pressed uncomfortably against her chest.

In the inky darkness, it was impossible to make out the shoreline to see if there was a safe landing spot. However, Carling was sure a landing would be out of their control even if they found a place. It felt to Carling as though the island was making that decision for them. She sat perfectly still, waiting, her hair blown back by the wind, her face dampened by the salty spray.

The boat jerked violently. Over the howling of the wind and crashing of the waves, Carling heard a scrapping noise followed by a loud *crunch!*

"A reef! We've hit a reef," shouted Kelfy, his voice cracking in terror as the boat tipped wildly to one side. "Hold on! We're going over."

To Carling, everything seemed to happen in slow motion. The boat dipped and rocked. Carling was tossed from her seat, her clutching fingers forced to let go of the gunwale by the violence of the boat's movement. For a long second, she was suspended in the cold, night air before plunging into the icy water. She rolled and tumbled, not knowing which way was up. Her head banged against the rough edges of the coral reef as she was pushed along under the surface of the water. Turning and spinning in a swirl of bubbles, she began to panic. Her lungs started burning...crying for air. She kicked her legs, cracking the top of her foot against the jagged reef. Still, she kept kicking, hoping to find the surface of the sea. She was encased in a swirl of foam with nothing but blackness beyond.

Her thoughts were a whirl of confusion that matched the bubbles. *Which way do I go? I don't know which way to go!* Flailing her arms and kicking her legs didn't help. *I can't make it!*

A vision of her mother, whom the Heilodius Centaurs killed while searching for Carling, appeared through the darkness. Her mother's arms were outstretched. She beckoned her, welcomed her. Carling reached out to her and kicked even harder. Her mother smiled and Carling felt warmth replace the bitter cold. She swam toward her mother in a frantic effort to reach her. Carling's heart ached to be with her again. How she had missed her mother this last year and a half. How she needed her now.

Just as she thought she was going to grasp the loving arms of her mother, something grabbed her hair and start pulling her...pulling her back. *No, let me be with my mother,* she thought. She watched, grief stricken, as the vision of her mother floated away.

Carling's face broke the surface of the water. She opened her eyes and looked into the panic-stricken face of Kelfy.

The Isle of Hy-Basilia

THE MID-DAY SUN WRAPPED its warmth around the five objects piled together on the beach. The wind covered them with sand until they looked like driftwood casually tossed ashore by the sea.

A curious seagull landed lightly on the highest hump. Turning its head from side to side, the large bird examined the flotsam for anything edible. A movement beneath its webbed feet sent the interloper back into the air with a squawk.

From the pile, an arm appeared. Then a head.

The head belonged to Kelfy.

The Duende shook his head as a lion shakes his mane, sending sand and seaweed flying in all directions. He gently rubbed the sand from his eyelids and face before opening his eyes just slightly, squinting in the bright sunlight. Kelfy pushed himself up to his knees and looked around. On his left was a palomino centaur, her long legs splayed out to one side, her eyes sealed shut by a crusty layer of sand. Her chest moved slowly up and down.

Kelfy turned and looked to his other side. Curled up in a ball next to his legs was a Duende girl, sand coloring her auburn hair yellow. Beyond her lay a chestnut Centaur with a stubby tail. Entangled in his long legs was a third Duende.

Kelfy jumped to his feet, as though suddenly remembering what happened. He turned to face the sea, his hands on his hips. He stood still, scanning the horizon for a long time. He took a deep breath and jumped over the palomino Centaur. Pumping his arms, he started running up and down the wet sand along the water's edge. "My boat! My beautiful boat. Where is my boat?" he yelled, his voice a mixture of sorrow and anger.

Kelfy's shouting awakened Carling who pushed herself up, brushed the sand off her eyelids and looked around. She filled her lungs with the warm, salt air and blew it out through her mouth. The crashing of waves on the shore brought memories crashing back to her mind. "Higson? Tibbals? Tandum? Kelfy?" she called out. Turning her head from side to side she saw Tibbals and Tandum. Her heart pounded against the Silver Breastplate.

She shook Tandum's large body where it lay beside her. "Tandum! Tandum! Wake up."

Tandum groaned and stretched his arms and all four legs. "Oh-h-h, I hurt everywhere," he said as Higson rolled away from the Centaur's legs.

Tibbals moaned and squirmed from where she lay on Carling's other side. "Are we alive?" she said, her hair falling over her face and muffling her voice.

"I think so," said Carling.

Just then, Kelfy ran up to them, carrying an oar. "My boat! My boat is nowhere to be found. This is all I could find," he said, shaking the oar in the air. He dropped to his knees on the sand and sobbed. "I promised Grandpopi I'd take care of it. And now it's gone," Kelfy wailed. "How will my family survive without that boat?" Kelfy bent over and pounded the sand. "My mother, my father, my brothers and sisters...they'll all starve!"

Watching Kelfy cry, Carling felt her heart ache with a mixture of sadness and worry. *No boat? Not only will Kelfy's family starve with no way to support themselves, but we are stuck on this island. Will we be forever stranded on Hy-Basilia? What will become of us?* She pressed her knuckles against her mouth. Angry at herself for her selfishness, she forced herself to think about Kelfy. *What will become of a fisherman without a boat?* She crawled across the sand and put her arms around Kelfy. "I'm so sorry, Kelfy," she whispered. "We'll help you... we'll figure something out."

"At least we're all alive," added Tibbals as she stepped up to Kelfy and patted his back.

"Yes, at least we're alive and in this together," said Higson, for the first time showing some concern for Kelfy. Soon all five of them were pressed together in a group hug, their faces showing both sorrow and fear.

Tandum, always the pragmatic one, was the first to disengaged himself from the circle. "We need to start exploring this island. The wizard sent us here for a purpose. We need to complete our quest before we worry about getting back."

Carling took a deep breath and looked up at Tandum. "You're right, Tandum. How should we begin?"

"We could split up and search for some sort of life," said Higson. "Maybe there are inhabitants on this island. Remember Fyzzle's story. He said there were Fairies here at one time. Maybe there still are."

"I'd like to suggest that we stay together," said Tibbals with a shudder. "If we split up, we may never find each other again."

"True that," said Carling. She turned back to Kelfy. "Maybe we'll be able to find another boat."

Kelfy scoffed. "I doubt that."

Higson patted him on the back. "At least we can try." Kelfy frowned and shrugged off the pat. Higson didn't notice or, if he did, didn't show it.

Side by side, the little group of castaways started walking down the beach. The sun was dropping to the west behind the hills barely visible on the mainland of Crystonia. Long yellow streaks shimmered on the tops of the rolling waves. Carling gazed over the water toward her homeland and wondered if she would ever set foot on it again. She blinked her eyes several times. The wall of fog that hid the island from view for all those years was gone. "The fog," she shouted. Everyone stopped and looked out to sea.

"It's gone," said Higson, so shocked his voice choked on the words.

They looked back and forth between the sea and each other. No one had an explanation.

With a shrug of her shoulders and a shake of her head, Carling turned back to face the way they were going. She sighed and started walking again.

Just before the sun set, they came to the end of the long, narrow beach. In front of them, waves rolled up and crashed against a high cliff wall, sending sea spray showering down around them.

"I guess this is as far as we can go along the beach. Shall we cut inland?" suggested Higson.

Carling scanned the area. Bordering the white sand was a thick jungle of vines, ferns and every kind of palm. Yet that seemed the only way to go. "I guess we have no choice," she said.

The jungle was extremely dense, and it did everything it could to be uncooperative. Pushing, tugging, and crawling, the explorers struggled to work their way inland. Wet leaves dripped on their heads and backs. Vines curled around their legs and gripped their ankles. Green, red, and yellow parrots swooped overhead, calling out in loud squawks. Monkeys leaped from branch to branch, scolding them with chattering sounds and clicking teeth. Steam rose from the moist ground, stinging their eyes, as the smell of rotting foliage and over-ripe fruit stung their noses. They worked their way around tall tabonuco trees whose pungent, oozing, white resin stuck to their clothing. Dense clusters of bamboo formed wooden fences without gates, stopping them in their tracks and forcing them to find new routes.

Tandum took the lead, breaking branches and holding back vines and palms so the others could pass. Step by soggy step, the five castaways made their way, ever so slowly, through the jungle, feeling more miserable by the minute.

Carling and her friends were not very far inland by the time the darkness of night enveloped them beneath the thick jungle canopy. They were so exhausted that they could barely lift their feet over a log or pull their feet out of the sticky mud. Feeling too tired and defeated to go any further, Carling suggested they stop for the night. The Centaurs and Duende curled up on the moist, soft ground and, without saying more than the briefest goodnights, fell asleep.

Carling awoke with a start. It was still night. She looked from side to side. Just barely visible in the darkness, her friends were sleeping around her, some balled up, others stretched out. She sighed and rubbed her hands through her curly hair, which was damp from the humidity. She felt the dry blood on her hair from the gash she'd received when she hit her head on the coral reef. The Duende touched the bump gently with her fingers. She was surprised that, until now, she had forgotten all about it.

As she pondered their strange situation, Carling became aware that something about the jungle was different. A chill of evil filled the air and a shudder shook her body. She looked around again, this time more slowly and carefully. She gasped. On the far side of the little clearing, two glowing red eyes were watching her. With a swirl of wind, the palm boughs shook and a transparent image began to materialize around the red eyes. The strange shape began to twist and turn and become more distinct until Carling could see an enormous black panther, its lips curling back to reveal sharp fangs. It growled, keeping her locked in its stare.

Carling's breath caught in her throat. She couldn't scream. She couldn't even move. She felt as though her body were under the wild cat's complete control. Her own fear enveloped her. *Is this the end then?* she thought. *Is this where we all die after all we've been through?*

Courage...I must call upon courage. The red stone on the Silver Breastplate grew warm. She gathered the strength to stand and, as she did so, extended her arms out to both sides. "I am not afraid of you. Well, maybe a little. But I will *not* let you hurt us," Carling said, her voice so calm it surprised even her.

The enormous, wild cat took one step toward her and her companions, growling and twitching the tip of its tail. With its red eyes still locked on her, it stopped, one front paw suspended in the air.

A little face appeared between the cat's pointed ears. Two small hands clasped the ears and pulled back, stopping the wild animal in its tracks. An odd creature climbed up on the cat's head and sat down, dangling his legs between the cat's eyes. He was only a foot tall. Wings whirled from their position on his back. His face looked young. His ears were pointed and stuck out from the shock of golden hair that covered his head. He wore tiny rings on his fingers and a necklace around his neck. Though she had never seen one, Carling had been told many fairytales as a child. She recognized the creature immediately as a Fairy.

"Well, what have we here?" the Fairy said in a squeaky voice, loud enough to awaken Tibbals, Tandum, and Higson. Tandum and Higson bounced to their feet. Tibbals cowered behind her brother. Apparently exhausted from fighting the storm and struggling through the jungle vines, Kelfy continued to sleep. The cat froze in place, his long tail twitching back and forth, his paw still poised for the pounce. A growl that sounded like tumbling rocks escaped his throat.

Carling kept her eyes on the Fairy. "W-who are you?" she stuttered.

"I was about to ask you the same thing. But since you asked first, I will tell you. My name is Wigglesworth. I am one of the guardian Fairies for the island of Hy-Basilia." Patting the cat, he added, "This is Grandle. He isn't very friendly. You're lucky I found you before he ate you for supper. Now, it's your turn. Who are you and where did you come from?"

"I am Carling from the mainland," Carling said, motioning toward the sea. "These are my friends who have come with me on a special quest. We have been sent here by the Wizard of Crystonia."

"The Wizard sent you here?" His eyebrows furrowed and his mouth twisted momentarily to the side in skepticism. "Well, I must say, *if* that's true, that changes everything. I will lead you to the Fairy King. He will know what to do with you." He pulled on one of Grandle's ears, causing the enormous cat to growl but succeeding in turning him around. "Follow me, won't you?"

CHAPTER 16

The Fairies' Valley

CARLING SHOOK KELFY. "WAKE up Kelfy. A Fairy has offered to help us."

"What? What did you say?" Kelfy yawned and rubbed his eyes.

"A Fairy has offered to help us," Carling repeated. "He said he will take us to the Fairy King."

"Did you say a Fairy? So there really *are* Fairies on this island? Great-Great Granpopi was right," he mumbled as he pushed himself up and stretched his sore muscles.

"Let's go," said Tandum, "before he gets too far ahead."

Wigglesworth led them to a trail that wove through the jungle, making the going much easier. Twinkling fireflies appeared on all sides, lighting the way. The Centaurs and Duende followed Grandle.

Wigglesworth alternated between riding on the cat and flying around them, talking excitedly as his wings whirled. His flitting around reminded Carling of the humming birds that populated the flower gardens in Centaur city of Minsheen.

"I must say, I am quite surprised to see you on our island. I have been patrolling the jungle for a hundred years and never found anything other than a few fighting Aardvarks. The Aardvarks only come out at night and I swear only then to cause trouble."

"Wigglesworth, we didn't expect to find Fairies on the island. We only heard rumors that you were here," said Carling as they walked along.

"You didn't know we were here? Why wouldn't we be here? It's our island after all," Wigglesworth said as he perched on Tibbals's croup, bouncing up and down with the rhythm of the Centaur's walk. He faced toward Carling. His little wings stretched out behind him.

"We didn't even know this island was here until we found it on a very old map," Carling said.

"I see. The fog. We were quite clever to hide it, weren't we?" said Wigglesworth with a smile. "It appears you forgot all about us."

"When did the Fairies come here?" asked Tibbals. She tossed her golden locks, which were still matted with sand, and looked back over her shoulder at the Fairy sitting on her hind quarters.

"We came hundreds of years ago, when the evil Wizard rounded up and cast the Humans out of Crystonia. We didn't like what was happening all over the land of Crystonia, what with the Ogres, Cyclops and..." Here he paused and looked back and forth between Tibbals and Tandum.

"Don't worry, Wigglesworth. We're good Centaurs," said Tibbals with a smile.

"Oh, yes. Of course, you are. Don't mind me. I'm still surprised that you're here. And I tend to talk too much," Wigglesworth said as he whirled his wings and lifted off Tibbals's back.

The pathway through the jungle was narrow but clearly defined. The large cat, so large he was half the size of the Centaurs, led the way, never looking back. His long legs covered the ground in great strides. His wide paws padded softly on the leaf-covered ground. As time passed, the darkness slowly lifted and the rising sun cast a warm light through the jungle. The colors of the dense, damp foliage changed from black to gray and, eventually, to every shade of green, dotted with bright splashes of yellow, red, orange, and purple flowers.

Carling looked around and admired the beauty of the jungle. She listened to the chatter of monkeys, the call of birds and the squawk of parrots. The jungle was alive and aware that they were there.

The little group continued deeper into the jungle, following the snarling cat. Carling was sure nothing would bother them with the cat around and was grateful for that.

"How far is it?" grumbled Kelfy at last.

"Oh, not much longer," said the Fairy cheerfully as he flitted among them.

Carling soon decided that "not much longer" feels a lot longer if you are a Centaur or Duende and walking instead of flying! By the time they broke out of the jungle, the sun was directly over their heads. Except for the Fairy, they were all tired and dripping with sweat.

Wigglesworth led them as they stepped out of the palms and vines and stopped them abruptly at the edge of a cliff. The view took Carling's breath away. Far below was an enormous valley, the centerpiece of which was a tall mountain made up of a collection of intricate spires. The valley circled the mountain as a moat circles a castle.

The sun sparkled off the tall spires of the mountain and flashed off the wings of what appeared, at first, to be only birds.

"My Fairy family and friends," Wigglesworth said with a smile and a sweeping motion of his arms.

Carling looked more closely and gasped. Hundreds of Fairies mingled with birds as they flew above the valley floor and around the central mountain. The sound of music reached Carling's ears. "Where is that music coming from, Wigglesworth?"

"The Fairies. They sing when they fly. If they want to go higher, they sing high notes. If they want to go lower, they sing low notes."

"But I didn't hear you singing when we walked through the jungle," said Tibbals.

"Oh, you noticed! How very perceptive of you. You see, the Fairies who are chosen to be the island guards must be trained to fly without singing. We must learn to just think the notes. It is very hard to do and takes a lot of practice. However, it is necessary for us to perform our clandestine duties."

Carling nodded. This made perfect sense.

With his tendency to get right to the point, Tandum said, "How do we get down there, being that we can't fly?"

Wigglesworth giggled. "Just leave it to me. I have a brilliant idea. But first, I must get dressed appropriately to enter the valley." The Fairy reached into a pocket of his pants and pulled out a tiny mask. Holding it up for them to see, he said, "We never enter the valley without covering ourselves properly." He positioned the mask over his little angular face. It completely covered his face except for two tiny eye holes. A straight line was painted where his mouth would be but, other than that, it was quite plain. He looked around at each of them. "We Fairies never show our faces. That enables us to keep our thoughts and emotions to ourselves."

"You hide behind masks?" asked Carling.

"Why is that?" asked Higson.

"Our faces are windows to our minds and hearts. Obviously, we don't want others to know what we are thinking or feeling. We like to keep our real selves hidden. Faces show way too much, don't you think?"

Carling blinked and turned to give Higson a questioning look. Higson returned the look by raising his eyebrows and shrugging. Their actions proved Wigglesworth's point.

"Now wait here until I return," Wigglesworth said. He lifted himself into the air, without singing, and swooped down into the valley. Carling quickly lost track of him among all the other Fairies.

"This is a beautiful place, but it's very odd," said Tibbals.

"I just hope they can help me find a new boat," said Kelfy.

"I hope they can help us find the Stone of Integrity so we can go home," said Carling.

"Of course," said Kelfy as he stepped up beside her. "That's the only reason I need a boat." He smiled at her.

Higson came up to her from the opposite side. Placing a protective arm over her shoulder, he said, "Don't worry, Carling. The Wizard knows we are here. He will not leave us stranded. He will see to it that you return to Crystonia." With a glance at Kelfy he added, "One way or another."

Before long, what appeared to be a multi-colored, pulsating cloud floated across the valley, straight toward them. When the object got close enough, they could see that what appeared from a distance to be a cloud was actually a large cluster of Fairies. Wigglesworth was in the lead, his mask still covering his face. Just as Wigglesworth said, all the Fairies around him were also wearing masks, face after face showing an expression that never changed.

Once the flock of Fairies reached them, the singing stopped and the Fairies landed softly on the ground or in the plants and trees around them.

One Fairy, larger than the rest yet still not more than a third of Carling's height, approached them. He raised his head slowly and looked from one to the other. True to its purpose, the expressionless mask effectively covered his thoughts. Carling was surprised at how nervous she felt not being able to read his expression. It never occurred to her before this moment how important reading faces was.

The Fairy placed his hands on his hips; his wings hung limp behind him. When he spoke, it was with a high-pitched voice. "So, Wigglesworth," he said, "this is an interesting collection of castaways you have brought to us."

"Yes," Wigglesworth said as he flew down next to him. "You can see for yourself that they are harmless enough."

"Harmless? How can we tell?" asked another Fairy, a permanent smile painted on her mask.

"The Wizard of Crystonia sent them here," said Wigglesworth.

"The Wizard?" said yet another Fairy with a frown painted on his mask. "How do you know?"

"They told me."

"And you believed them?"

"Well...yes. Perhaps I shouldn't. But just look at her face," said Wigglesworth as he flew up to Carling and patted her cheeks. "Isn't she adorable?"

"Adorable or not, can we trust a face?"

"Isn't that why you wear masks?" asked Carling.

Immediately Fairies started talking and flitting around.

"She's right. Of course you can trust a face. That *is* why we wear masks," said one.

"Perhaps they've just mastered control over their thoughts and emotions so they don't need masks."

"That could be true, you know."

This went on for a while as the Fairies debated back and forth.

Wigglesworth flew up in the air, whirled around and raised his hands. "Quiet everyone." The Fairies became silent. "*I* think she's telling the truth. So, I propose we take them to the Fairy King."

"Good idea. Let him be the judge," said the large Fairy who had spoken first.

"If they are lying, he can throw them in the pit," said the Fairy with the smile on her mask.

Carling's eyes widened. "The pit?" she said.

"Yes," said one Fairy with a giggle. "And you'll never get out."

"Oh, dear," moaned Tibbals.

Carling felt the Stone of Courage grow warm, magically giving her the courage she needed. "We have nothing to worry about since we *are* telling the truth."

"See," said Wigglesworth to the other Fairies, "she's very persuasive, isn't she? Now, let's get to work!"

The Fairies started singing a song of high notes as the entire group lifted off their various perches. They disappeared into the jungle. When they returned, they carried thick vines. Several of these they wrapped around Carling's, Higson's, and Kelfy's bodies. Many more were wrapped around Tibbals's and Tandum's bellies. With wings whirling and voices singing high notes, the Fairies lifted the travelers off the ground.

Tibbals squealed in fear and pressed her eyes tightly shut.

Kelfy shouted. "Hey, set me down! Set me back down!"

Carling gritted her teeth and clasped the vines tightly.

As soon as the Fairies carried them past the edge of the cliff, the little winged creatures started singing songs with low notes. Immediately they started slowly descending toward the valley floor.

Feeling more secure, Carling looked around. "Tibbals," she said, "open your eyes. It's beautiful." For, indeed, it was. The valley was as lush and green as the jungle but much more cultivated and orderly. Tiny houses were surrounded by large, manicured flower and vegetable gardens. Little shops, painted in bright colors and topped with red roofs, lined the curving streets of the evenly spaced villages surrounding the mountain. Fairies dashed about singing their high and low songs, often stopping in mid-air to gawk at the odd cargo their fellow Fairies were carrying.

Tibbals opened one eye a tiny bit...a *very* tiny bit. She quickly closed it again. "I can't look, Carling. We're too high up."

Tandum and Higson, on the other hand, watched their journey with wide-eyed wonder.

As they got closer to the mountain, Carling realized that its odd shape was not natural. It was the result of careful sculpting. "Are we going to the mountain?" she asked the Fairies who were carrying her.

"Yes. That's the castle of the Fairy King," said a Fairy who was holding on to one of the vines wrapped around Carling.

"Who created such a beautiful castle?" Carling asked.

"Oh, we did...all of us. We have been carving it out of the marble mountain for as long as anyone can remember."

"Yes, we just keep carving and carving," said another Fairy.

Carling looked more closely at the castle. To one side, she saw several Fairies hovering in the air around one spire. With tiny chisels and hammers, they chipped at the stone, creating a flower-and leaf-covered vine that wound its way up the column.

"It will never be finished," said a third.

"Why not?" asked Higson, overhearing the conversation from where he dangled in the air nearby.

"Because we don't want it to be. Legend has it that if we ever finish, we will all die," said the first Fairy. "No one wants to find out if that is true or not!"

Carling looked up into their faces to see if they were serious, but with their masks on, she couldn't read their expressions. *Hum-m-m, I guess the masks really do work,* she thought, *but they kind of bother me.*

The Fairies carried Carling and her friends to the south side of the mountain castle. Here, two long rows of turrets extended from the castle on either side of an arched bridge marking a grand entrance leading to a set of gilded doors. The Fairies lowered Carling and her friends to the ground at the end of the bridge, untied the vines, and freed them from their harnesses.

Wigglesworth flew around them, his mask sitting slightly askew. "Line up neatly. We like order here."

Carling took the lead. Higson and Kelfy each hurried to get behind her. Kelfy won. Higson frowned and stepped in behind him. Tibbals was next, and Tandum brought up the rear.

"Very good. Very good. Now, I'll take you to see the Fairy King. He will know what best to do with you," said Wigglesworth.

CHAPTER 17

The Fairy King

WIGGLESWORTH SPUN AROUND, HIS wings a whirl of blue and green, and led them across the arched bridge. They walked in a straight and orderly line between the two rows of sparkling columns. Between each set of columns, a railing made of vines woven together like lattice kept them from falling off the bridge. Carling looked over the decorative railing and noticed the bridge spanned a moat filled with turquoise water. Several white swans glided silently over the top of the water. A few Fairies rode on the backs of the swans. The side of the moat nearest the village was covered with dark pink fuchsias. Carling could smell their sweet aroma. It made her smile. The other side of the moat was bordered by the straight stone walls of the castle. Thick moss grew up the sides of the wall, painting the interlocking marble stones a deep green.

When they arrived at the golden doors, Wigglesworth pulled down on a long, red, velvet cord.

A deep, loud, *bong* sounded above their heads. The large doors swung inward, aided by dozens of Fairies, all dressed in red.

The Duende and Centaurs followed Wigglesworth inside. As soon as they were through the doorway, the Fairies pushed the doors shut. Carling and her friends stopped and looked at the scene before them, their eyes wide, their mouths agape. Everything about the great room in which they now stood bespoke not only great craftsmanship but immense wealth as well. Carling turned in a slow circle, looking at everything around her. The floor sparkled with inlaid jewels. The white marble walls were decorated with enormous paintings, mostly of Fairies in nature, hung in ornate, gilded frames.

One painting caught Carling's eye. It was much larger than all the other paintings. No Fairies were depicted in this painting. Instead, it was an eerie depiction of a lonely path heading into a thick forest of mangrove trees. It held Carling's attention for a long moment and filled her with an odd mixture of fascination and fear. The painting seemed to have a strange power over her, as though it was trying to pull her in. With great effort, she turned away to continue surveying the room.

High over their heads was a ceiling of concentric, intersecting arches. The plaster between each arch was painted in one of many bright colors. Hanging from the highest arched dome was an enormous, gold chandelier from which red, green, and purple stones dangled from invisible wires. Candles covered the chandelier and cast a warm, yellow light throughout the room.

Fairies, dressed in bright colors, flew around the cavernous room, humming and singing, the sounds echoing off the walls and adding even more excitement to the space. Little doors, set in the walls at all heights, opened and closed as Fairies came and went. Of course, each Fairy face was covered with a mask.

"Oh-h-h, this is beautiful," gushed Tibbals.

"I've never seen anything like it," said Carling in a reverent whisper.

"They don't make houses like this in Duenton," said Higson.

"I've seen better," scoffed Kelfy as he glared at Higson. Higson responded with a sneer.

Wigglesworth held himself in the air in front of them in the same way a swimmer treads water. In a self-satisfied tone of voice, he said, "Do you like our castle?"

Carling was quite sure he already knew the answer since, without masks, he could read the looks on their faces. But she responded anyway, for the Fairies' creation deserved the praise. "Oh, Wigglesworth, it is truly amazing. I don't know what to say. Words can't adequately describe it," she said.

Wigglesworth seemed pleased as he said, "I'm so glad you like our little home. Now, if you'll wait here, I will ask the Fairy King if he has time to meet with you. Frankly, if he can't or won't, I don't know what I'll do with you," he added with a chuckle. Through the holes in his mask, Carling saw that he winked an eye.

Wigglesworth spun around and flew up to the highest door in the room. Carling and her companions watched as he tapped on the little door before disappearing behind it once it opened.

"I hope he doesn't expect us to go up there," said Kelfy.

"For someone as adventurous as you," said Higson with a snort, "you sure don't sound very brave."

Kelfy gave him a nasty look. "I'm fine sailing on the water, unlike *some* Duende. It's flying through air I'm not used to." He folded his arms across his chest and turned his back on Higson with a huff.

Tandum attempted to appease both Duende. "I can't imagine that he would," he said. "First, Tibbals and I would never fit through that tiny door."

"And *none* of us can fly up there," added Tibbals.

While they waited, several Fairies stopped to examine the strangers, most saying nothing, just looking them over. Their masks, some painted with smiles, others with frowns, hid their true thoughts.

One Fairy flew down and stopped in front of Carling. She was dressed in a flowing pink dress. Her legs were covered with pink stockings, her feet with tiny pink shoes. In her hair were numerous pink bows of different sizes. Her mask was painted with pink circles for cheeks and a pink mouth in a pucker. "Are you a Duende?" she asked in a squeaky voice that was muffled slightly by her mask.

Carling nodded. "I am."

"Humpf. I've never seen one of your kind before. You're much bigger than I imagined."

"I've never seen a Fairy before I came to Hy-Basilia," Carling said, giving her a warm smile.

"Why aren't you wearing a mask? I can tell what you're thinking just by looking at your face."

"Is that bad?"

"Of course it's bad. How do you expect to keep anything secret? And what if you want to tell a lie? Everyone would know right away."

"I guess I wasn't planning to keep any secrets or tell any lies," said Carling, feeling a bit befuddled.

Just then, Carling heard a door bang open above their heads. She looked up in time to see Wigglesworth fly out the door he previously entered. Behind him, a large, round Fairy flew into the great hall and, singing a song with low notes, flew down to where the visitors stood. He landed softly on the bejeweled floor, right in front of Carling.

This was obviously the Fairy King for a tiny crown rested on his head between his pointed ears. Tiny spectacles rested on the nose of his mask. His clothing was made of gold brocade fabric that shimmered in the light of the hundreds of candles on the chandelier above. His white hair hung in ringlets down to his shoulders. Carling dropped to one knee and bowed her head. Higson, Kelfy, Tibbals, and Tandum did the same.

"Your Majesty," Carling said.

The king nodded in acknowledgement. "Please stand." Carling and her friends did so. The king continued. "So, you are the ones who have penetrated the fog. Your arrival explains why the protective wall has disappeared. I am told you have come to my island at the instruction of the great Wizard, Vidente."

"That's correct," Carling said.

"Tell me," the king asked, "why did he send you here?"

"I have been sent to gather the Stone of Integrity."

The king sang several high notes as his whirling silver wings lifted him into the air. "The Stone of

Integrity? *You* have been sent to gather the Stone of Integrity?"

Carling dropped her head to her chest, feeling the Stone of Courage and the Stone of Mercy grow warm against her body. "Yes, Your Majesty, I have."

"Does this mean you possess the Silver Breastplate for which we have been waiting for so long?"

"I do," said Carling, confident the Wizard would approve her revealing as much.

Kelfy, upon hearing this, jerked his head around and gaped at Carling in shock. He had been told only about a quest to gather some sort of stone. The Silver Breastplate was never part of the conversation.

The king's mask covered any feelings he might have. "Can you prove this to me?" he said, still hovering in the air in front of her.

"I can. I am wearing it even now," she said as she unlaced her cape and unwrapped her tunic, revealing the beautiful, intricately carved Silver Breastplate covering her blouse. The green Stone of Mercy and the red Stone of Courage twinkled in the candlelight. Carling was sure that the artisanship reflected in the breastplate would impress the Fairy King.

Kelfy gasped, his hands flying to his mouth. Tandum gave him a nudge, "There is much you don't know about her," he whispered out of the side of his mouth.

"So I see," Kelfy whispered back.

"You see, Your Majesty, all I have told you is true," said Carling.

The king peered at the Silver Breastplate for quite a while, his eyes squinting. When he spoke, his voice was filled with excitement. "I must say I am pleased that the Wizard has selected one of our Fairy cousins to be the future ruler of Crystonia. I would have detested having to work with the Ogres or Cyclops. The Centaurs," and one of his tiny eyes winked at Tibbals, "would have been much more pleasant. But a Duende! A Duende! Nothing could be better. You are half Fairy, you know."

"Are you able to help me find the Stone of Integrity?"

"I am the only one who *can* help you for I am the one who has hidden it."

CHAPTER 18

Rivals

THE FAIRY KING INSTRUCTED Wigglesworth to take the travelers to a large house in the closest village, a house large enough to fit three Duende and two Centaurs. Turning to Carling, he said, "I will come in a few days to give you your instructions. In the meantime, refresh yourselves, rest, and relax." He started singing a song with high notes and lifted toward the ceiling. The Fairly King flew to the highest door and disappeared behind it.

Wigglesworth did as he was instructed. The house in the village to which they were directed was, indeed, large enough for all of them. The front door even allowed the entry of Centaurs. Inside were colorful, soft cushions set around a low table. A fireplace on the far wall provided both heat and light. Empty chairs and benches, placed in a semi-circle around the stone hearth, invited them to gather around. Even Tibbals and

Tandum found sofas large enough for them to fold their front and back legs and lie down.

Fairies brought food and clean clothing for each one. Several female Fairies filled tubs in a back room, one large enough for a Centaur, one just perfect for a Duende, with warm water and plenty of bubbles so both Carling and Tibbals could bathe.

"Ah-h-h," said Tibbals, as she stepped into the scented water. "I needed this."

"Me, too," said Carling with a giggle.

"Yes, you did," said Tibbals.

Carling immediately sent a splash of bubbles her friend's way. Tibbals returned in kind. Both girls laughed with delight as bubbles flew around the room.

The next day, Carling and her friends relaxed, ate delicious meals of fruits, cheeses and breads, and read books with titles such as *It Isn't Easy Being a Fairy, My Mask is Better Than Your Mask,* and *Ogres, Cyclops and Other Beasts to Avoid.* It was a rest sorely needed by all of them.

The second morning, Carling awakened to a beam of sunlight shining through a crystal suspended from a silver thread and dangling in front of her window. It painted a broad rainbow on the wall directly across the room. She sat up and pulled her knees to her chin, wrapping her arms around her legs. She smiled as a feeling of contentment, a feeling that had eluded her for quite a while, flowed through her.

She sighed and glanced down at the Silver Breastplate sitting on the floor beside her bed. The Stone of Mercy and the Stone of Courage twinkled with their own light. The intricate designs, molded into the silver of the breastplate, sparkled. As she looked at the breastplate, the feeling of contentment vanished, squashed by the weight of the responsibilities that she carried.

The future queen threw back her blankets and stood up. She dressed quickly, placing the breastplate over a soft blouse, latching it on the sides. This she covered with a rough outer tunic. She sucked in a large breath, filling her lungs, and felt her chest press against the breastplate...a constant reminder of her future role.

Tip-toeing past the sleeping Tibbals, she opened the door and slipped into the main room of the cottage. All was silent. It seemed that no one else was awake. Carling hurried across the room and out the tall front door. She stopped on the stoop to breathe in the sweet scent of flowers as a gentle breeze kissed her face. The young Duende turned her head slowly from side to side, trying to decide which direction she should go. With a shrug, she decided to walk straight ahead.

Carling soon discovered that the village was built around a tiny town square that wasn't a square at all. It was perfectly round. All the homes and shops were built on concentric circles moving out from the center of the village the way water ripples when a stone is tossed into a lake. Carling walked straight toward the town square. She stepped onto the manicured lawn, shuffling her feet through the thick, green grass. She stopped in the center to gaze up at a statue of a Fairy perched on the top of a tall column. The Fairy sat with one leg dangling down. The other knee was bent. Her elbow rested on her knee and her chin rested on her fist as though thinking about something very important. Carling cocked her head and smiled, pleased that the

Fairy portrayed was not wearing a mask, and tried to imagine what was causing her to be so pensive. She walked around the statue and continued forward, leaving the park and the rows of shops and houses behind.

Beyond the village was a neat, weed-free field of cabbages, each plant larger than the Fairy who must have planted it. Carling stepped carefully over the rows so as not to damage the perfect plants. It was what lay beyond the field that was beckoning to her. A thick clump of evergreen trees, pines mostly, formed a border along the edge of the cabbage field. Soon, she found herself running and leaping over the rows, so eager was she to get to the forest. She tossed her hair back and turned her face toward the sun, its rays covering her with a blanket of joy.

Carling entered the forest between two identical pine trees that stood guard like sentries in front of a castle. Immediately, the air felt cooler and the gentle breeze disappeared, leaving the forest still and quiet. Carling stopped and looked around. The ground was soft and covered with pine needles. She started walking forward, her feet sinking into the springy ground.

Beyond the shelter of the aromatic pine boughs, ferns found their desired environment. Growing close together, they provided a thick undergrowth reaching to Carling's waist. She pushed them from side to side as she walked through, making her own path.

Eventually, she came to a clearing within a circle of trees...a perfect meditation spot. She sat down, cross-legged, and closed her eyes. The silence dissolved into a chorus of forest sounds...birds calling, insects chirping, little animals scurrying. Carling listened with the appreciation one would give a symphony.

Carling pulled up her knees and wrapped her arms around her legs. She rested her chin on her knees and sighed. Her thoughts turned to her parents and the life she once knew in her little village of Duenton, the village of her childhood. It was a childhood filled with peace and happiness. Life was so much simpler then. There were no walls around her village in those days. Tears stung the backs of her eyes and she pursed her lips, trying to keep the tears in. She had promised herself that she would not let others see her cry any more...not even Higson. She saved her crying for nighttime...when she was alone, curled up beneath the covers. But here...here she was alone. She let a tear trickle down her cheek.

Her reverie was broken when she heard her name.

"Carling! Carling!"

Her eyes popped open and the corners of her mouth dropped. She recognized Kelfy's voice. Carling brushed the tear from her cheek.

"Over here," she said reluctantly, sad to have her meditation time interrupted.

Kelfy crashed into the clearing, perspiration dampening his hair and dripping from his forehead. "Carling! I've been looking all over for you. Are you alright?" He slid to his knees right in front of her and clasped her hands in his.

"I'm fine, Kelfy. I just went for a walk."

"Oh, thank goodness. I was so worried about you." He dropped her hands and wrapped his arms around her.

Carling stiffened slightly, not relishing a hug by a sweaty boy even if he was only trying to be nice.

Just as he did so, Higson rushed into the clearing. "Wh-what are you doing?" he stammered, a look of both shock and hurt on his face.

Kelfy turned his head and smiled at Higson. He did not release his hold on Carling. "I found her," he said, giving Higson a self-satisfied smile.

Carling pushed Kelfy back. "Kelfy thought I was lost."

Higson scowled. "We all did," he said. "Kelfy, I told you to stay at the cottage...that I would find her." He looked at Carling with both sadness and anger in his eyes.

Kelfy laughed outright. "Oh, so you did. But I don't remember anyone putting you in charge." Kelfy shifted his position so he was staring directly at Higson.

Sensing the tension that destroyed the peace and beauty in the clearing, Carling scrambled to her feet. She stepped between Kelfy and Higson, holding up her palms. "It's alright, both of you. I do appreciate your concern but, as you can see, I'm fine. Next time I want to go for a walk, I'll be sure to let someone know where I'm going." The undercurrent of dislike that she felt flowing between these two bothered her. She didn't understand where it was coming from and didn't like it. She had also never seen this type of behavior from Higson and didn't know what to make of it.

"Or take me with you," said Kelfy as he stood up beside her and placed an arm around her shoulder. "I can protect you."

Higson turned away with a huff and marched back through the forest.

The King's Instructions

A FEW DAYS LATER, Carling and her friends heard a knock on the door. Higson got up and went to the door, opening it wide. The Fairy King flew into their house, followed by Wigglesworth. The two Fairies alighted on the soft cushions of a chair by the fireplace in which a warm, glowing fire flickered.

"Well, dear Carling and friends," began the king, "it is time to give you the instructions you will need to find the Stone of Integrity. The day for recovering the stone is nearly upon us, and we dare not miss it or we will have to wait an entire year before we have the opportunity to gather it again."

"Then please tell us what we need to do," said Carling as she sat in a chair directly across from the two Fairies.

"The day after tomorrow will be the Winter Solstice celebration...the shortest day of the year, don't you know," said the king.

Carling and her companions all nodded. They were familiar with the Winter Solstice for it was a day of celebration all over the land of Crystonia.

The king continued. "There will be parties and games in every village throughout our valley."

Wigglesworth rubbed his hands together with a silly grin on his face and a twinkle in his eye. "It's the best day of the year," he said in his high, squeaky voice.

"You are welcome to join in any of these festivities for part of the day. However," at this point the king's voice became very solemn, "before the sun reaches its highest point, you must go to the castle. There you will find a painting of a path in a mangrove forest."

Carling sucked in her breath. She remembered seeing the painting and feeling the strange power it seemed to send into her. She felt her skin tingle and her breath get short. With some effort, she forced her attention back to what the king was saying.

"When the sun is at its highest point, you may step through the painting onto the path. But only when the sun is at its highest, and only if you do not blink." The king stopped and looked from one to another as if trying to determine if his instructions were understood. All the travelers' faces held a blank expression as if it was *they* who were wearing masks.

Carling was having a hard time believing what she had just heard. "Step *into* the painting?"

The king nodded. "But *only* when the sun is at its zenith, and only if you do not blink," he repeated.

Carling's eyes blinked involuntarily.

The king continued. "Once you enter the painting, you will still have a challenge ahead of you to retrieve the stone. I had to hide it in a place that no one else would find. And it won't be easy for you, either."

The king started singing a song with high notes and lifted off the chair. "Oh, and one more thing. I am sending Wigglesworth with you. He will have further instructions for you once you make it through the painting. Um...*if* you make it through the painting."

Several times over the next two days the little group of travelers discussed the odd assignment. Everyone expressed concern at the strange message the king gave them. But they also voiced their willingness to accompany Carling.

"Imagine stepping into a painting. That sounds impossible," said Tibbals.

"We've been doing a lot of impossible things," said Tandum, "like sailing through a band of vicious Adaro."

"And getting carried through the air by Fairies," added Kelfy with a shiver. "But I'll do it for you, Carling."

The little Duende girl was touched when Kelfy said he was willing to go. "Oh Kelfy, that is so kind of you to offer, but you have already helped so much. You really don't need to go."

Higson jumped in. "You've already done more than you bargained for," he said, facing Kelfy. "You agreed to sail across the Swirling Sea and into the fog. You don't need to do any more."

"I can handle this," said Kelfy, folding his arms across his chest and lifting his chin. "Don't worry about me."

Higson frowned and turned away.

The day of their journey arrived and any bravado that had been previously expressed was replaced by a thick silence.

Carling and Higson decided to get rid of some of their nervous energy by going to the village to see the celebrations. The Winter Solstice dawned bright and clear...a perfect day for the holiday festivities.

Carling and Higson left the house before the others. As she walked beside her friend, Carling's thoughts kept drifting to the journey on which they must embark in just a few hours. "What are you thinking about, Higson?" she asked.

Higson stopped and took her hand. "I'm just wishing you and I were back at home, hunting in the forest. I can handle that. I don't like the sound of all this. Magic always scares me a bit. What if we step into the painting and can't get back out?"

Carling bit her lip and nodded. "I was worrying about that, too. But the Fairy King must have thought of that and made a way for us to escape once we find the stone."

"*If* he wants us to get the stone. Remember Shim? He didn't want to give up the Stone of Courage. What if the Fairy King is just like him?"

Carling took a deep breath and let it out with a huff. She bit her lip and tried to suppress the fear she was feeling. The Wizard's words came back into her head. *Courage is not the absence of fear. Courage is conquering that fear in order to always do what is right.* She put her hand over the red Stone of Courage, comforted by its warmth. "Let's get this done and get back home."

Once they reached the center of the village, they found the festivities in full swing. Music from harps and flutes filled the air. The aroma of freshly baked breads and pastries tickled their nostrils. Tiny Fairy children were dashing about giggling with glee, flying around banners and streamers of colored ribbons.

All the Fairies were dressed in their fairy finery. No longer were their faces covered with plain masks. The masks they wore to the festival were beautiful works of art. Some were covered with colorful feathers. Some were decorated with leaves or flowers. Others sparkled with gems and crystals. Each one seemed to be more grand than the last.

An endurance flight had begun several hours before Carling even arrived in the town square. Fairies were racing around the mountain castle. The leaders were just crossing the finish line, with barely enough wind to sing their final notes. The audience cheered and threw flower petals into the air to greet the competitors.

Carling's interest was piqued by a game going on near the village square. Fairies, still in their childhood, judging from their small size, were playing a fast-paced game with balls and hoops. Two teams of Fairies, dressed in matching uniforms, were tossing balls, catching them in the air, and throwing them through one of the many hoops that circled the square. She noticed that the teams were awarded more points if the ball went through one of the smaller hoops and fewer points if it went through a large hoop. Carling and Higson cheered as they watched the scores climb.

As the game continued, Fairy bands started playing rousing music on horns and drums and a giant string instrument played by four Fairies plucking at the same time. Fairy couples began dancing both on the ground and in the air to the pounding beat.

Tibbals, Tandum, and Kelfy soon joined Carling and Higson. Carling smiled, glad to have their company. Kelfy was frowning as he approached, and stepped between Carling and Higson.

"I never like to miss a party, you know," said Tibbals. Carling noticed that her giggle carried an uncertain edge to it.

"We just needed to keep our minds off today's adventure," added Tandum as he swished his stubby tail.

"Adventure?" Kelfy snorted.

Even with all the festivities, for Carling and her friends, the morning seemed to crawl by. Carling kept glancing up at the sun but it never seemed to move. She felt restless and kept moving around the village, trying to enjoy the music, smells and colorful sights. "At least the Fairies are having fun," she said.

Tibbals bent over and gave her a sympathetic hug.

At last, Carling noticed that her shadow extended just a few inches from her feet, signifying the sun's imminent arrival at its zenith.

Tandum observed it, too. "It's time to go, Carling," he said, as gently as he could.

"Where is Wigglesworth?" asked Higson. "I thought he was going with us."

"Perhaps he is already at the castle," said Carling.

She guessed correctly for, as soon as they arrived at the arched bridge, they saw Wigglesworth flying back and forth with apparent impatience. "There you are, at last. You certainly know how to give a Fairy an upset stomach."

Wigglesworth led them into the mountain castle. As soon as they entered, Carling's eyes went immediately to the large painting directly in front of them. It was, indeed, the same painting that captured her attention on the day of their arrival. It was the painting of the path entering the thick, dark, mangrove forest; the painting that called to her.

Carling felt her heart beat more rapidly. No matter how frequently in the last year and a half she had been in danger, she was still not accustomed to it. She always knew by the pounding of her heart and the shivering of her flesh the immense difference between a dream and reality. As odd as the Isle of Hy-Basilia was, it was no dream. And this painting was no ordinary painting.

She walked up to the painting, her hand outstretched. Her fingertips touched the rough texture the thick layers of paint created on the canvas. It felt just like any other painting. It didn't seem like it would be possible to walk right through it. *And if I can walk through it, what will I see on the other side?* she asked herself.

She didn't have much time to study the painting or wonder about the magic that it held, for Wigglesworth called for their attention. "It's time to step through the painting," he said. "And I must remind you, *do not blink.* If you blink, you will not be able to go through. Carling, you take the lead. I will take the rear. Now go! If we wait we will miss the zenith."

Carling sucked in her breath and noticed that her eyes desperately needed to blink. She blinked several times, then clenched her teeth and concentrated on holding her eyelids open. She took one more deep breath and, with the Stone of Courage burning against her chest, stepped up to the painting.

No longer was the painting a hard, impenetrable object. To Carling, it felt more like stepping into a wall made of soft, supple water without getting wet. In one more step she was *through* the painting. It all happened so quickly, she'd hardly realized it happened at all. She was shocked to find herself standing on the very path depicted on the canvas surrounded by the very same mangrove trees.

Behind her, the rest jostled for position and their turn to step into the painting. Higson rushed up to follow Carling. As she disappeared, he readied himself by taking a deep breath and lifting his foot. Just as he was moving forward, his eyes held tightly open, he was pushed...hard...from behind. Losing his balance, he fell forward and...blinked.

With a chuckle, Kelfy stepped past him and through the painting.

CHAPTER 20

Inside the Painting

CARLING TOOK A FEW steps forward just as Kelfy, followed by Tibbals and Tandum, stepped onto the path behind her.

A few seconds later, Wigglesworth flew through the painting. "He blinked!" the Fairy exclaimed. "Your friend, Higson, blinked."

"What?" said Carling, furtively glancing all around in a hopeless search for Higson. "What happened to him?"

"He's fine, just ran into the painting as though it was made of stone. He will have to wait for us," said Wigglesworth as he brushed off his shirt and pants.

"Oh, no," moaned Tibbals. "How will we do this without him?"

"Oh, we'll be fine," said Kelfy. "We don't need him. I'm here to help you."

Tibbals frowned but Carling smiled. "We're glad for that, Kelfy," she said as she reached out and squeezed his hand. Kelfy looked in her eyes and returned the smile. "But I'm sad that Higson won't be here. He has always been my support."

"Don't worry. You have me to support you, now," Kelfy said, lifting her chin and winking at her. Tibbals's frown darkened.

Wigglesworth interrupted and took command. "We will need to follow this path to a channel of water. A boat will be waiting for us."

"A boat? See?" said Kelfy as he looked back and forth at the others. "I told you I could be a big help." A wide smile spread across his handsome face and he winked at Carling again.

"Yes. Thank goodness you are here," cooed Carling. She returned the smile and felt her heart flutter just the tiniest bit. Then a feeling of guilt flowed through her as she thought about leaving Higson behind. Turning her face to look up at Wigglesworth, she said, "Is there anything we can do to get Higson here?"

"No, nothing. I told him not to blink! I can't help it if he did." Wigglesworth spun around in the air and started flying up the path.

Carling shrugged, swallowed her disappointment, and resigned herself to continuing without Higson. She hurried down the path behind Wigglesworth.

"Carling," called out Tibbals from behind the young Duende, "let me carry you."

Carling, who was already having trouble keeping up with Wigglesworth, took advantage of the offer and quickly climbed up on Tibbals's back.

Tandum nudged Kelfy, a bit too roughly perhaps, sending him stumbling to one side. "Would you like to ride?"

Catching himself, Kelfy shook his head. "I don't want to ride any more than I want to fly. I'll keep my feet on the ground, thank you very much."

"Suit yourself," snorted Tandum as he trotted past. Kelfy started running as fast as his little legs would carry him as he struggled to keep up.

The Centaurs trotted and Kelfy ran through the tunnel formed by the mangrove trees, which were growing dense and thick on both sides of the narrow pathway, sending their leafy branches arching over their heads. Carling heard animals moving through the brush and crawling up into the trees. Even though she could hear them quite clearly, she couldn't see them.

It kept getting darker and darker the further into the forest they went. The air got hotter, thicker and moister. Carling felt her auburn curls sticking to her face and neck and wished the air was a few degrees cooler. She felt Tibbals's body getting sweaty between her legs. She squinted her violet eyes, attempting to see Wigglesworth better as he flew, bobbing up and down, in front of them.

As they moved deeper into the jungle, the foliage became so dense they couldn't see the Fairy or the path. Tibbals stopped. Tandum bumped right into her. A minute later, Kelfy bumped into Tandum with an "Oomph."

"Sorry," Kelfy said. "I can't see a thing."

"Wigglesworth! Wigglesworth," called Carling. "Come back. We can't see where we're going."

Wigglesworth flew back. "Oh, sorry. I didn't realize your eyes were so weak." The Fairy flew to the top of the trees and with a "crack" broke off a leafy branch. With a snap of his fingers, the leaves started glowing.

Though the leaves sent out a warm, magical, yellow glow like a candle, they weren't consumed the way a candle's wick and wax would be by a flame.

"Oh, that's much better," said Tibbals as she reached out her hand and took the makeshift torch. She held it high above her head so all could benefit from the light.

Wigglesworth led them for what seemed like an entire day. How long, Carling couldn't tell for sure. The darkness never changed. At long last, the Fairy stopped at the edge of an inky black canal and removed his mask. His eyebrows were knitted together below his tangles of golden hair. He ran a jerky hand through his hair to get it out of his face, his mouth formed into a frown. "This is where the journey begins," he said, his voice trembling slightly.

CHAPTER 21

The Canal

"BEGINS?' SAID KELFY, WHILE huffing and puffing. "I thought we were already on it." He bent over, resting his hands on his knees, and tried to catch his breath.

Wigglesworth's mouth turned up. "I'm sorry to have worn you out so. I had to bring you to this waterway. We must follow it to where the Stone of Integrity is hidden."

Wigglesworth snapped his tiny fingers and a small, flat boat became visible in their circle of light and floated to the shore. The boat held two seats. Tucked beside the seats were two oars.

"As you can see," Wigglesworth continued, "the boat is too tiny for the Centaurs. But it will be the perfect size for our two Duende. It appears the Fairy King knew all along who would be coming to retrieve the stone."

"What are *we* to do?" asked Tandum, his hands on his hips and his brow furrowed, looking as though he was offended at being left behind.

"I would suggest that you wait right here," said Wigglesworth, trying to keep his voice patient. "If Miss Carling returns with the stone, I trust she will be quite tired and will need assistance getting back. You can be very helpful at that time."

"*If...?*" began Tibbals. She was immediately silenced by a stern look from her brother.

Carling didn't like the sound of that either. Her face turned sour to match her mood. The thought of continuing this journey without Tibbals, Tandum and Higson was not to her liking. This made her more grateful than ever for Kelfy's presence.

Wigglesworth brushed aside their concern with a wave of his hand, though the tightness of the muscles in his tiny, angular face reflected that he harbored concerns himself. "The Stone of Integrity is at the bottom of a large lagoon. We will reach the lagoon, which sits at the far side of this mangrove forest, by rowing through this channel. It is important we reach the lagoon while it is still very dark for we will be looking for special signs in the water that will only show up in the darkness."

"What signs are those?" asked Carling as she wiped the perspiration away from her eyes.

"When you disturb the water with your oars, the water will sparkle. At first, it will appear to sparkle in white and green, but as we get closer to where the Stone of Integrity is located, the sparkles will turn first to yellow, then to red. But when the flickers of light appear to be purple, we will know that we are right over the stone."

Carling stepped up to the tiny boat and stopped. The first time she'd sailed in a boat was when she left Madiera to come to Hy-Basilia. That boat had been ten times bigger. She felt her body get rigid and her palms get clammy. Her thoughts went to the storm and her brush with death beneath the surging waves. She remembered the vision of her mother beckoning her. Her stomach pinched and she felt her eyes sting with tears. How she missed her parents and wished they could help her now.

Kelfy stepped up beside her. "Let me hold it steady while you climb in." With one hand, he held the little boat. The other he extended to her.

Relief washed over Carling as she wiped her palms on her cape and took his hand. She felt a tingle flow through her body at Kelfy's touch, and she let out her breath and smiled at him. Trying to be as graceful as possible, she carefully stepped into the boat, but it rocked wildly to one side. Carling squealed as she dropped down and clasped the sides for balance.

"Keep your body low and move to the other end," Kelfy ordered.

Grateful to have Kelfy's expertise, she loosened her grip on the sides of the boat, kept her torso bent over, and shifted forward, trying to keep the boat from rocking too much.

Once she was settled, Kelfy followed. The small vessel bobbed as he dropped into place, but Carling did her best to help balance it by holding very still right in the middle of her seat.

Sitting on the bench, Carling noticed a coil of thick vines at her feet. *I wonder what that is for?* she thought. Before she had time to ask, the Fairy flew over her head.

"Let's get started," said Wigglesworth. With a whirl of his tiny wings, he buzzed over to Tibbals, took the glowing branch out of her hands, and propped it up in the front of the boat. "Both of you take an oar and follow me," he said.

Dipping their oars in the water, Carling and Kelfy pushed off and glided away from the shore, leaving Tibbals and Tandum to wait in the dark. Carling glanced back. She thought how afraid she would feel to be left behind in the dark. "We'll be back as soon as we can, Tibbals and Tandum," she called out.

"Be safe," said Tibbals, her voice floating away in the darkness.

The rowing didn't go terribly well at first. Carling's inexperience hindered their progress, sending them in circles.

"You're dipping too deeply," said Kelfy, irritation in his voice. "Skim across the top with your oar perpendicular to the water. Let's row together. Listen to me...stroke...stroke...stroke."

Learning to keep the boat in line took some practice. Carling tried her best to follow Kelfy's instructions, but she had trouble keeping her oar perpendicular to the surface. The little Duende often ended up splashing and pounding the water instead of stroking.

Carling felt herself getting more and more frustrated. She wished Kelfy could just take both oars and do it himself. She expressed this desire through clenched teeth. However, Kelfy explained that a narrow boat such as this was designed for two to row together. "You'll get it. Just keep trying," he said.

Eventually, they began working as a team and the little boat slid forward across the surface of the water. "Ahh, that's much better," said Kelfy, "Not too deep. You've got it now." Carling extended her oar forward, lowered the edge of the paddle slightly into the water, and pulled back. The boat slipped silently forward.

It was a warm, sticky night. Fireflies popped in and out of view as Carling and Kelfy pulled their oars through the water. Even though she couldn't see them, Carling could hear signs of life all around her. The rustling of leaves above them indicated the movement of birds and animals. Insects buzzed, attracted to the light from their little torch. Frequent splashes told her fish were taking advantage of the insects' presence to fill their stomachs.

Outside their little ring of light, Carling couldn't see anything. What the little torch did reveal within that circle did little to raise Carling's comfort level. The channel was narrow. The water beneath them was inky black. The mangrove trees on either side grew tightly together, forming a virtual wall. Their branches intermingled overhead to form a tight ceiling. The air around them smelled of fish and rotting vegetation. It was so still, Carling couldn't feel even the tiniest breeze to offer relief from the humidity.

As they rowed, Carling kept her eyes on Wigglesworth and the dark line of the channel in front of them. They struggled to keep up with the Fairy. Before long, Carling's shoulders began aching each time she pulled the paddle through the water. On occasion, she asked Kelfy to switch sides to give her arm a rest. That worked quite well if they did it together.

They were gliding along through a particularly narrow part of the channel when a large fish jumped out of the water and landed in the boat at Carling's feet. Startled, Carling screamed and pulled her feet back, tucking them beneath the seat. She started batting at the fish with her oar.

Wigglesworth stopped flying ahead and turned around. Kelfy stopped rowing.

"What's the matter?" said Kelfy.

"There's a huge fish in the boat!"

Leaning over her shoulder and seeing the fish flopping about made Kelfy laugh heartily. Carling glared at him but resisted the urge to shove him for laughing at her. She didn't see what was so funny.

As soon as Kelfy caught his breath, he said, "Hold still. I'll take care of it. Fish are my specialty." Keeping his body low, he worked his way over her seat to the front. As quick as a cat, he grabbed the fish and threw it back in the water. "There you go, although I must say, it goes against everything I believe in to throw back such a big fish."

Carling let out a loud sigh of relief and pivoted in her seat to face Kelfy. "Thanks, Kelfy. Sorry I screamed. It just surprised me."

He gave her a gentle hug. "Oh, that's all right. I think you're very brave. In fact, I think you're just perfect."

She didn't see the roll of his eyes. Rather, Carling noticed the flutter in her heart. She felt her face get hot. She enjoyed the attention from this handsome young man and was glad he couldn't see the blush in her cheeks in the darkness. She cleared her throat, turned back to the front of the boat and grabbed her oar. "Let's get going," she said as she dipped the paddle into the water too deeply.

At long last, the channel opened into a huge bay. Overhead, thousands of stars twinkled in the sky. Wigglesworth circled back and landed on the bow of the boat in front of Carling.

"Here we are," he said with a smile. "Now the real adventure begins."

"I hate it when you say that," grumbled Kelfy.

"Carling and Kelfy," said Wigglesworth from his perch in front of Carling, "you must pay careful attention to the colors that appear in the water when your oars break the surface. As I mentioned, the water in the bay is luminescent. The organisms in the water will glow when disturbed. The colors will change as we get closer to the location where the Stone of Integrity rests. When you see the water sparkle with tiny, purple lights, stop."

Carling and Kelfy slapped their oars on the water. Carling watched the water, curious to see what would happen. Her mouth dropped open when she saw the water sparkle with little, white, lights just as Wigglesworth said. "Oh! That's so beautiful," she said.

"Yes, it is," said Wigglesworth with a smile. "The Fairy King would only choose a beautiful hiding place for the stone."

Carling and Kelfy paddled with more earnest. They headed out toward the middle of the bay. At first, the light in the water was just white, then, gradually the lights changed to green. "The colors have changed," said Carling with excitement.

"Keep going," said Wigglesworth.

Soon the lights turned back to white. "Oh no," moaned Kelfy.

"Change direction," said the Fairy.

Kelfy turned the boat to the right by back paddling and pointed the bow away from the center of the bay. "This is going to be harder than I expected," he said. "This is a mighty big bay."

"We'll find it," said Carling. "I know we will." She felt a strange sense of confidence and an equally strong sense of calm run through her. "We will, because we are supposed to."

After several more twists and turns, the sparkles in the water turned green again and, after what seemed like a very long time, yellow then red.

CHAPTER 22

Finding the Stone of Integrity

WE'RE GETTING THERE, SAID, Carling, her voice filled with excitement. "I see red lights in the water."

"You're right there," agreed Wigglesworth as he hung over the front of the boat staring into the black water that twinkled with little flashes of red. "Just look how many red lights there are. I think we should keep going in this direction."

Kelfy bit his lip as he concentrated on keeping the boat going straight while he and Carling worked together to keep moving forward.

With a jerk of her paddle, Carling stopped rowing. "Wigglesworth, did you see that? The color of the sparkles just then...it was purple. Look!" She swished her oar through the water, causing the water to sparkle. "Purple!" she said.

Wigglesworth looked over the side. "Do it again."

Kelfy stopped rowing and rested his oar on his lap.

Carling dipped her oar and swished it back and forth. Purple lights sparkled in the water.

"I see it!" Wigglesworth and Kelfy exclaimed together.

Carling looked from one to the other, smiling broadly. "So, here we are." Then her smile changed to a frown. "But now what?"

"Now you dive down and get the stone," said Wigglesworth.

Carling's heart jumped to her throat. "How deep is it?" she asked as her body shuddered.

"I don't know," said Wigglesworth, "but that's what the vine is for."

"That vine?" Carling asked, pointing to the coiled-up vine in the bottom of the boat. "What good will that do?" Carling knitted her eyebrows together and the corners of her mouth dropped back into a frown.

"It will enable you to breathe under water." Wigglesworth hopped down to the floor of the boat and picked up the end of the vine. Carling noticed that it was hollow like a tube.

Kelfy worked his way up to Carling's seat so skillfully the boat didn't even rock. "Would you like me to dive down to find it?" he asked, placing an arm gently around her shoulder.

Carling looked at him and smiled, truly grateful for the offer. "Thank you, Kelfy. But I think this is something I need to do myself."

She bent over and picked up the end of the vine. Placing it to her mouth, she sucked in a lung-full of air. The air that filled her mouth and throat tasted salty but at least it was air. She looked up at Wigglesworth. "Alright, I guess this will work."

Leaning over the side of the boat, Carling stared at the smooth black surface of the water. Her thoughts went to the other times she'd buried herself underwater to save someone. First, she struggled to save the leader of Pik's band of Fauns from drowning in the raging river in Manyon Canyon. Just a few days later, she dove into Lake Mantle with Tibbals to save Dalt, a Heilodius Centaur. As a result of her actions, both Pik and Dalt were now loyal friends. The thought occurred to her that, in a way, this dive into the deep was to save her entire kingdom.

Carling reached down and shook her hand in the cool water, hoping to see purple lights twinkle. With a sigh of relief, she watched as the disturbed water sparkled with a bright purple color. They were in the right spot. This was the place they were sent to find.

The red Stone of Courage burned against her chest. Carling pulled off the cape and her boots. She pushed her auburn curls out of her face and sucked in a deep breath before putting the vine in her mouth. She stood on the seat and glanced from Kelfy to Wigglesworth. "Here goes," she mumbled, the vine between her teeth, and dove into the silent, black water.

Once in the water, Carling quieted her pounding heart and forced herself to breathe through the vine. It didn't come naturally so she stretched out her arms and legs and floated long enough to get in a rhythm of breathing through her mouth. The water was warmer than she'd expected, but its saltiness caused her eyes to sting.

Holding still caused the purple lights to disappear, and Carling found herself surrounded by darkness, making it even harder for her to keep from panicking.

She struggled to remain calm enough to think. *Be calm. Be calm*, she told herself. She firmly quelled the lump of panic that filled her chest and forced herself to breathe slowly.

Holding the tube in place with one hand, Carling practiced until she mastered the art of breathing through the hole, sucking in life-giving air. She swished her head from side to side and pushed her hair out of her face with the other hand. Every movement disturbed the water enough to cause the purple lights to twinkle in welcoming response. She did a half somersault in the water and started pulling her arms and kicking her legs to go deeper. Initially, her body was surrounded by purple lights. But the farther down she swam, the fewer lights appeared in the water until there were none at all. She was enclosed by the complete and terrifying darkness of the water.

Carling stopped swimming downward and spun around, trying to figure out which way to go. She looked first one way, then another...searching for purple lights to guide her. Just as she was about to give way to her fear of the penetrating darkness and follow the vine back up to the boat, she saw a tiny sparkle below her. For a moment, it was there, then it disappeared. She convinced herself that it had been a figment of her imagination. But then she saw it again...a tiny twinkle of light far beneath her. Trying not to blink, she rolled her body over and started swimming toward the spot where she had seen the light.

Down through the inky black water she glided, the water getting colder and thicker with each stroke. As the pressure from the water became greater, Carling found that sucking air through the vine became more difficult. Her lungs began complaining, wanting more air. Long, winding plants tried to catch her arms and legs as she neared the bottom of the bay, but she kept staring at the spot where the tiny light now alternately appeared and disappeared, working her way closer and closer.

Just as she was about to reach the light, an underwater current pushed the seaweed and plants over it, blocking her view. Frantic, she pushed aside the plants and ran her hands through the sandy soil. Her fingers brushed against something hard and warm. With both hands, she scooped up the object. Bringing her hands to her face, she opened her palms. Nestled in one hand was a beautiful purple stone. Her heart beating with excitement, she folded her fingers over her palm, enclosing the stone.

In that moment, the thick, black water started to glow with a radiant, white light. Carling swished her head around toward the light, pushing the strands of her hair out of her face. Suspended in the water like a shifting cloud in the sky, the Wizard smiled at her, the lights around him glimmering as softly as a breath of spring air.

Though Carling could not see his lips moving, the Wizard's voice floated into her mind. "The Stone of Integrity is now in your keeping, Carling," he said. "With the power provided by this stone, you will develop the ability to live with honesty and truth. A leader who serves her people with integrity will garner their trust. Never betray that trust for trust is very difficult to earn back once it is lost."

There was a long pause in the Wizard's message as though he desired her to absorb the importance of what he just said. Carling continued to float in the water, moving her arms rhythmically from front to back. Barely breathing, she kept her eyes on the apparition that was the Wizard and waited.

After several minutes, Vidente's voice entered Carling's mind again. "With practice, it will help you, my young queen, discern the motivations of others as well. Though you may yet suffer betrayal by those close to you, it will help you learn to look into people's hearts. Only there will you see who they are. Be true, Carling. Be true to yourself and to others. No longer hide who you are."

The Wizard vanished and the waters became inky black again. Carling looked from side to side, but the Wizard was gone. She looked down at her hands and sucked in a deep breath from the vine. The stone was gone as well! She wanted to call out to the Wizard to tell him she had lost the stone, but then she heard his voice in her mind again. "The stone now rests where it belongs," his voice said. His final words drifted away like a summer breeze. "Remember who you are."

CHAPTER 23

Unmasked

REACHING THE SURFACE WAS easier than Carling anticipated, and soon her head broke through the water, sending purple sparkles out in all directions. "Hey, I'm here," she said to Wigglesworth and Kelfy, who were leaning over the other side of the boat.

Tipping the boat wildly, Kelfy and the Fairy moved over to her side of the little craft.

"Did you find it?" asked Kelfy.

"Um-m-m, could you pull me in first? Then I'll tell you."

Carling lifted up one arm and Kelfy clasped it tightly, pulling her up and over the edge. She landed in the bottom of the boat with a "Humpf!"

"Well? Did you find it?" Kelfy asked again.

Carling lifted her wet tunic. Nestled in its place in the Silver Breastplate, the purple stone sparkled in the cold night air.

"Wow!" exclaimed Kelfy and Wigglesworth together.

"That must be a very valuable jewel," added Kelfy.

"More valuable than money can buy," said Carling. "When temptations come my way, it will give me the power to always live with integrity."

Kelfy's face reflected his confusion, but he simply shrugged and handed Carling her dry cape to wrap around her shivering body.

By the time Carling, Kelfy, and Wigglesworth rowed back to where Tibbals and Tandum were waiting, the sun was high overhead. A tiny bit of light was worming its way between the leaves on the mangrove trees, turning the grove from black to gray.

"You're back at last," said Tibbals with a delighted squeal.

"Did you find the stone?" asked Tandum.

Carling's smile gave him the answer.

Carling kept her body low as she worked her way to the edge of the boat, not wanting to fall in the water. She'd spent enough time in the water for the day. Tibbals helped her climb out. "Oh, Carling," she said, "I'm sorry I didn't bring a brush to fix your hair."

Carling's thoughts rarely ventured to her auburn curls, which now hung in wet strings all over her head. "That's alright, Tibbals," she said. "You can fix me up when we get back through the painting." A thought entered her mind and she turned to Wigglesworth. "We *can* get back through the painting, can't we, Wigglesworth?"

"Oh, of course. Nothing to it. Just don't blink."

When they arrived at the backside of the painting, Carling was surprised to see that from this side it appeared to be a representation of the palace room in which it hung. She slipped off Tibbals's back and stepped up to the canvas, touching it gently with her hand. Looking back, she asked, "Is it time? Can I pass through?"

Wigglesworth nodded.

Keeping her eyes wide open, she turned around and stepped into the painting.

The first thing Carling saw was Higson curled up on the floor to one side of the painting. He was snoring softly. She stepped over to him and gently shook his shoulder. Startled, he looked up with hooded eyes. Then a smile of relief spread across his face. "You made it back," he whispered.

Carling smiled and nodded.

"Did you find the stone?"

Carling, smiling even broader, nodded again.

Higson jumped up and threw his arms around her. "You did it, Carling! You are one step closer to becoming the queen!"

Soon all of Carling's companions had successfully stepped through the painting into the palace. While Tibbals was her usual excited self as she told Higson about their adventure, Tandum remained quiet.

Noticing this, Carling walked over to her friend. She reached up and took his hand. "What's the matter, Tandum?" she asked.

Tandum started to say something but then shook his head, pursed his lips, and swished his short tail.

"I'll tell you what the matter is," said Kelfy as he stepped up beside them. "We all want to go home, but

Tandum and I are worried about how we will return to Madiera without a boat."

"A boat? A boat, you say?" said Wigglesworth, flying up while adjusting his mask to cover his face. "I'm sure we can help with that."

Kelfy's face brightened as he opened his eyes wide and raised his eyebrows. "You can? How?"

"Why, we'll build one, of course! I'll go speak with the Fairy King immediately."

Wigglesworth flew upward with a whirl of his wings and disappeared inside the highest door. Instantly, the little door opened again and the Fairy King flew out. Singing low notes, he zoomed to the floor of the palace and stopped in front of Carling. "Do you have it? Do you have the Stone of Integrity?"

Carling unwrapped her cape, revealing the sparkling purple stone set into the Silver Breastplate.

"Wonderful! Wonderful," the King said as he clapped his tiny hands. "Today will be a new day on the Isle of Hy-Basilia. Integrity has been brought back to our world." The king put one hand to his mask and lifted it off his face.

Wigglesworth gasped and fell backward onto his miniature rump. "Your Highness," he sputtered, "you removed your mask."

"Yes. I hid the Wizard's Stone of Integrity. But when I hid the Stone, I also ceased living with integrity. I convinced...no *commanded*...everyone to hide their true selves behind these masks," he said, holding the mask between two fingers and shaking it. "The arrival of Carling with her fresh, honest face, and her willingness to sacrifice everything to find the next Stone of Light, made me realize I have been wrong. No longer will the

Fairies of Hy-Basilia hide behind these masks. We shall have integrity as a people. We shall be true to ourselves and to others." He smiled at Carling. "Thank you for helping me realize my mistake. It was through watching you that I regained the courage to do what is right." He bowed to Carling.

Carling raised her eyebrows, doubting she had done anything. "You honor me with your words, Your Highness," she said. "I shall try to live up to your opinion of me. Thank you."

The king flew into the air, his handsome face wearing a broad smile. "Wigglesworth, call all the Fairies to the palace. I have an important announcement to make." Winking at Kelfy, he added, "And it seems we have a boat to build."

Wigglesworth looked at Carling with a twinkle in his eye and a silly grin on his uncovered face. He rubbed his cheeks. "This is going to take some getting used to!"

CHAPTER 24

Building a Boat

OVER THE NEXT FEW days, the Fairies, their masks removed, set about building a boat under Kelfy's direction. Carling could now tell immediately which Fairies were happy about the assignment and which were not. It was nice to know.

Carling smiled as she overheard one conversation.

"Hey Flossie, can you help me with this board?

"Sure, be happy to."

"No, you're not. I can tell just by looking at your face. But I appreciate the help anyway."

With a lot of hard work, and even more Fairy magic, the boat began to take shape. Kelfy was beside himself with excitement. Carling enjoyed watching him bounce around as he pointed here and pointed there, called out instructions, and examined the Fairies' progress. While Higson, Tandum, and Tibbals worked alongside the Fairies, Carling spent most of her time meeting with the

Fairy King, though she helped with the building when she was able.

One morning, Carling and the Fairy King were seated in the shade of a short palm tree, watching the construction of the boat in the little bay curving out in front of them. The black panther named Grandle was curled up next to Carling, allowing her to stroke his sleek coat.

As she petted Grandle, Carling thought about their return trip to Madiera across the Swirling Sea. She gazed over the sea to the south where the shoreline of Crystonia lay, just visible on the horizon. Now that the wall of fog had been lifted, she wondered if the fishermen in Madiera could see Hy-Basilia.

"You are troubled. I can see it in your face," said the king.

"I'm just thinking about our return trip."

"What are you thinking?"

"Can the Duende of Madiera see Hy-Basilia now?"

The king looked out to the sea and nodded. "Yes, I suppose they can, now the fog has lifted."

"Why is it gone?" Carling asked.

"You broke the spell, my dear. You and your friends. Once the curtain of fog was penetrated, it dissolved. Perhaps forever. I don't know. But I do know that the Fairies will no longer hide behind masks *or* a wall of fog."

"Will that cause you a problem?"

"We still have these awful Adaro, don't forget. They take their responsibility guarding the island very seriously." He turned and looked at her, a mischievous grin on his face. "They are pretty nasty creatures, aren't they!"

Carling chuckled. "True that," she said.

"Speaking of the Adaro, I have often wondered how you managed to sail past them," said the king.

Carling reached down the front of the Silver Breastplate and pulled out the magic flute.

The king tilted his head to one side, his face reflecting skepticism.

Reading his expression, since he no longer wore a mask, Carling said, "It's a magic flute. It puts the Adaro to sleep."

"To sleep? Amazing. Where did you get it?" asked the king.

"From the witch named Hilgalda."

The king reared back, fluttering his wings wildly. "That old hag? Is she still around?"

The Fairy King flew up in the air singing high notes until he was directly in front of Carling. Staring deeply into her eyes, he said, "Beware of her, my dear. Beware of her."

CHAPTER 25

Over the Sea in Madiera

WHILE CARLING AND THE King sat on the beach enjoying Hy-Basilia's perpetual summer, winter arrived in Crystonia with all its frigid glory. Cold winds whipped up the sea foam, forming icicles on the dock and boats. Snowflakes spun in circles like dancing white tornadoes. Gray clouds hung low over the water as though too lazy to rise. For the fishermen of Madiera, this changed little except necessitating two sets of long underwear and a heavy coat.

Pikins, the Faun, had spent each day since Carling set sail keeping an eye out on the Swirling Sea. He was the first to notice the lifting of the fog the day after his friends set sail. "Fyzzle, look!" he exclaimed, before realizing the blind fisherman couldn't see where he was pointing. "Oh, sorry," he added, lowering his hand, duly embarrassed.

"What is it, youngster? What do you see?"

"The fog. It's gone. And, what's more, I can see an... Is it...? Can it be...? An island!"

"Hy-Basilia," Fyzzle whispered with awe. "So, it does exist." The old fisherman scratched the whiskers on his chin and smiled.

Pik was sure the disappearance of the fog was a good sign. *Surely*, he thought as he gazed out to sea, shading his eyes with his hand, *that means Carling has reached the island.*

The lifting of the fog and the ensuing appearance of the island caused quite a stir among all the inhabitants of Madiera. Fishermen ran through the village streets, telling everyone about what they saw. Soon, everyone was talking about the island that no one knew existed. Shopkeepers left their shops and scurried down to the docks to see for themselves. Some felt it was an evil omen of bad things to come. Others believed just as adamantly that it was a good sign, the opening of a new age of discovery.

Over the next few days, when no major changes came to disrupt the daily routines of the Duende in Madiera, imaginations calmed and speculations ceased. Life and work had to go on, after all. Everything returned to normal in the little fishing village. Fishermen returned from the Swirling Sea with their daily catch but were still unable to get past the Adaro to reach the island. Customers still arrived from inland to buy the bounty from the sea. Decks still needed swabbing. Nets and sails still needed mending. The smell of fish and the sting of salty air still filled the village.

Each day, Pik's cloven hooves carried him from the inn, through the village and over the rough wooden planks of the pier, where he spent the day helping Fyzzle mend nets. Each day started with eager anticipation that today would be the day the voyagers would return. Each night was filled with disappointment that they had not.

More than two weeks of boredom passed for Pik as he waited for the return of Carling and her friends. The Faun's only entertainment was spending time with the old fisherman. He enjoyed listening to tales of life on the sea. However, all of that changed one day. While walking through the village toward the docks, his cloven hooves clicking on the cobblestone streets, Pik overheard a conversation that caught his attention. He strolled past a table where several Ogres were fighting over the last remaining salmon. The Faun looked up just in time to see two Heilodius Centaurs approaching the Ogres. One was tall and thin with a dark brown equine body and black tail. Black hair covered his human head. The other was much shorter and stockier with a pale-yellow body and matching tail and hair. But both wore the tell-tale black and silver shirts of the Heilodius soldiers.

Pik felt his heart catch in his throat and he slipped into an alleyway between two stores. Hidden in the shadows, he peeked around the corner of one building and watched as the Centaurs stopped beside the Ogres.

"Hello, comrades," said the shorter of the two Centaurs.

The Ogres grunted and continued playing tug-o-war with the slippery fish body of the last salmon.

The taller of the two Centaurs cleared his throat. "Have you been here long?"

Not to be bothered, the Ogres merely grunted again before growling at one another.

"I'll take that as a 'yes,'" said the tall, dark Centaur, a condescending tone in his voice and look on his face. He turned to his companion and rolled his eyes.

"Have you, by chance," said the short Centaur, "seen any Duende riding on Centaurs? That isn't normal, you know."

The Ogres grunted yet again, but the Duende fisherman who was selling the fish interrupted his efforts to save his goods from being ripped apart by the Ogres. "I have. I saw a young girl and boy riding on two Centaurs entering the village several days ago."

The Centaurs immediately turned their backs on the Ogres to face the fisherman. "Several days ago, you say?" the tall Centaur said. "When, exactly?"

"Oh, I don't know," said the fisherman while wresting the salmon out of the large hands of an Ogre. "I can't be sure. Maybe it was weeks ago."

"First you said 'days,' now you say 'weeks,'" said the Centaur, his face now twisted with impatience. "Which is it, man?"

Shaking his head and straightening his display of fish the merchant said, "Hard to say. Each day is just like the previous one around here."

"Are they still here?"

"I haven't seen them for, as I say, *several* days, perhaps as much as two weeks. Look, I have my hands full here. I can't keep track of everyone that comes and goes."

"Where would they have gone?" asked the short Centaur.

"Your guess is as good as mine," said the Duende, turning his attention back to his customers and his salmon, which was rapidly becoming suitable only for stew. "Visitors come and go from Madiera every day."

"Well, let us know if you see them again." The tall Centaur slapped a gold coin on the table.

The fisherman froze and gaped at the coin. His mood instantly changed. "Surely, surely, I will," he said with a toothy smile as he released the salmon and grabbed the coin, stuffing it in the pocket of his apron.

As the Centaurs turned and began to move away, the fisherman added, "Oh, kind sirs, one thing just occurred to me."

The Centaurs stopped and looked back over their shoulders swishing their tails with impatience.

"They had a Faun with them. A Faun with a red beard," he said as he stroked his chin getting bits of fish in his own beard. "The Faun is still here. He's spending his days with the old, blind fisherman, Fyzzle."

Pik withdrew deeper into the darkness of the alleyway, his heart pounding wildly. He jerked his head from side to side, trying to decide which way to go so he could get past the Centaurs without being seen. He dashed to the end of the alley and found an exit to his right behind one of the buildings. His mind raced and a sense of panic caused him to sweat so much that his long forelock stuck to his forehead. He hurried down the next narrow street, looking for Pernilla Persdotter's apothecary. *My beard...I need to get rid of my red beard.*

Keeping his head bowed and letting his ears flop forward to conceal his face, Pik dashed between shoppers and villagers.

"Hey! You there! You Faun!"

The shouts were coming from behind him. Pik's heart leaped to his throat and his blood chilled in his veins. He knew the voices. They belonged to the Heilodius Centaurs.

"Come back here, Faun!"

Pik didn't turn around. He paused for only a second, one cloven hoof held suspended above the ground, while he glanced from side to side, looking for an escape. To his right an alleyway between two shops offered some hope. He turned and ran as quickly as his two cloven feet would take him. Spurred on by fear and the adrenalin pumping through his body, he covered the distance to the rear corner of the buildings in a flash and skidded to a stop. In front of him was an old fence made of vertical boards placed side by side. The fence was connected to both buildings and completely blocked the passageway. Behind him, Pik could hear the clopping of hooves running toward him. He gulped. Examining the fence more carefully, he noticed a loose board hanging askew a few Centaur tail-lengths away. He ran to the board and, with a grunt, pulled as hard as he could. It came free so suddenly that he fell backward, sprawling on his back in the dirt. But he didn't take the time to assess any damage to his goat or human body. Instead he jumped up and tried to dive through the narrow gap in the fence, but his goat haunches, being wider than the rest of him, proved a bit too wide for the gap .

"Hey, there he is! He's getting away. Stop him!"

The angry, threatening, words were enough to give Pik the extra strength he needed to squeeze through the gap, leaving behind patches of skin and hair on the boards of the fence.

Pik didn't look back, nor did he check his stinging haunches. He simply ran, pumping his arms and gulping for air, until he reached Pernilla's shop. Glancing both ways, Pik put his hand on the doorknob. With one last look, he opened the door and slipped silently inside.

Later that afternoon, a Faun with a neatly trimmed gray and black beard to match his gray and black forelock and a fresh pair of pants covering his haunches, walked gingerly out of Pernilla Persdotter's apothecary. While his appearance was radically different, his name was still Pikson.

Pik walked slowly, limping on both legs, toward the wharf, trying not to draw attention to himself. He looked straight ahead and avoided eye contact with any of the villagers and out-of-town shoppers. He even hummed a little tune, trying to act as though he were simply enjoying a leisurely stroll through the blustery, cold winter day, and arrived at the dock just as the last of the fishing boats were coming in for the day. The whirl of activity reminded him of the beehives in the trees that filled the Forest of Rumors. Everyone was busy. No one noticed him. Pik felt a rush of relief flow through him.

When he arrived at Fyzzle's shack, he noticed the old man's chair was empty and lying on its side. A net the old Duende had been mending the day before, sat in a jumbled pile beside the chair.

Pik's racing heartbeat caused a pounding in his head that drowned out the sounds of the crashing waves and howling wind, and he dashed into the shack. Sitting on the floor in the center of the little room was Fyzzle. His hands were bound behind his back with rope. His feet were tied together at the ankles. The old fisherman's face was covered with rough burlap and tied around his neck. His cries for help were muffled by the fabric.

"Fyzzle!" cried Pik as he dropped to his knees beside the old fisherman and frantically started struggling to untie the ropes that held the old Duende fast. "What's become o' ye? Who done this to ye?" He pulled off the fabric, uncovering a swollen and bloodied face. When the old man turned his head, a large bruise, ugly with purple and blue, appeared on the side of his head. Pik gasped.

Fyzzle slowly shook his head and rubbed his wrists and ankles. His sightless, milky eyes were swollen shut. "Two Centaurs came to my shack looking for you and Carling," his said, his voice cracking. "When I wouldn't tell them anything, they grabbed me and beat me. I thought I was done for. But, instead of finishing me off, they just dragged me in here and tied me up. I was hoping you would come soon. What took you so long?"

"I be very sorry, old friend," Pik said as he finished untying Fyzzle. "I be trying to disguise meself, I chanced to hear two Heilodius Centaurs asking 'bout Carling in the village. One o' the shopkeepers told 'em 'bout me...that I be with Carling...so Pernilla helped me change me appearance. I had no idea any harm would come to ye."

Fyzzle pushed himself up, wobbling as he did so. Pik leaped forward to help him to a chair.

"Thank you," said Fyzzle. "Well...at least I'll mend eventually. Not much worse than a battle with a stormy sea, I wager. But I'm concerned about Miss Carling. What kind of trouble has she gotten herself into?"

Over the next little while, Pik told Fyzzle all he knew about the Silver Breastplate. He felt the old man should know considering what he had just been through. The Faun recounted the efforts by the Heilodius Centaurs to prevent Carling from gathering all the Stones of Light and becoming the Queen of Crystonia. Fyzzle listened while staring toward the sea and not blinking. He nodded, on occasion, but never smiled.

When Pik finished, Fyzzle sighed. "It seems my grandson has gotten involved in something bigger than he ever could have imagined."

"I be sure Carling be grateful fer his help," Pik said.

"Yes, yes," Fyzzle said, gingerly touching the bruises on his face. "But we need to find a way to keep them safe once they return."

Returning to Madiera

A FEW DAYS AFTER the Centaurs attacked Fyzzle, Kelfy and his makeshift crew piloted their Fairy-made boat back toward the docks of Madiera. Sitting in the bow of the boat, Carling felt her pulse quicken with excitement as the docks and Fyzzle's shack come into view. "There it is," she said, standing up and pointing ahead.

Suddenly, Kelfy turned the boat sharply to the right. Carling fell to one side and caught herself just before falling over the side of the boat.

"Hey!" shouted Higson as he grabbed Carling. "What are you doing, Kelfy?"

"See that flag flying over Fyzzle's shack?"

Everyone turned and looked. Yes, indeed. Just as Kelfy said, a red flag, on a pole attached to the little shack, was flapping in the winter breeze, clearly visible against the threatening lead-gray sky.

Carling turned back and looked at Kelfy. She noticed his wrinkled forehead. His mouth was pinched. His eyes were fixed on the flag as he continued struggling to turn the boat against the current that wanted to push them into shore. Her stomach tightened. "What does it mean, Kelfy?"

"It's a warning from Fyzzle. There's danger. He wants me to land in the western cove."

"The western cove?" asked Tandum.

"Yes. That's our secret rendezvous spot if ever it isn't safe to dock at Madiera. He will be there waiting for us."

Carling kept her eyes on Madiera as Kelfy turned the boat to their right and began sailing parallel to the shoreline. From where they were in the sea, the village didn't look dangerous. She watched boats approaching the dock. She saw tiny specks that were Duende milling around on the wharf. Everything looked perfectly normal. But now, the anticipation she felt at completing this part of her quest by arriving at Madiera, was gone. She scrunched up her face, trying to bury the disappointment that now replaced her excitement. Then she thought of Pik. *If there is danger in Madiera, is Pik involved? Is he safe?*

Kelfy sailed the boat around a point of land that protected Madiera's harbor. Jagged rocks erupted from the sea floor like giant claws trying to grab them, but Kelfy skillfully guided the boat between them. Rolling waves tipped the boat first one way, then the other. Carling, Higson, Tibbals and Tandum held on tightly while Kelfy worked the rudder and boom. Carling glanced back at him several times, awed by, and grateful for, his strength and skill.

After rounding the rocky point jutting out into the sea, they found themselves in much calmer waters. Kelfy turned the boat toward the shore. The cold, winter wind blew them swiftly forward. The young fisherman shifted the sail to bring them into a little inlet. The front of the boat jerked to a stop as it hit the sand, and Kelfy jumped out of the stern of the boat. Keeping his hand on the rail, he waded through the water and grabbed a rope on the bow. Higson and Tandum followed him into the water and helped pull the boat ashore. Soon, it was resting on the sandy beach of the cove.

Carling and Tibbals stepped out of the boat, Carling wobbling a bit as she adjusted from the rocking of the boat to stable ground. She rested a hand on Tibbals's equine shoulder. Looking up, she gasped. Coming toward her was a Faun with a neatly trimmed gray and black beard, guiding Fyzzle. She squinted as she peered at the Faun. When he waved, she slowly lifted her hand and gave a hesitant wave back.

"Carling! It be me. Pik!"

"Pik?" Carling said, trotting up the sand to meet him and the old fisherman. "What happened to you? You look so...so different."

Pik bent down and scooped Carling up into a hug that left her feet dangling in the air. "I be so glad to see all o' you. I be worried sick about you, Missy."

"We're here. We're fine. But what's going on?"

Pik lowered Carling to the ground and told her about the Heilodius Centaurs searching for her in the village. He also told her about the attack on Fyzzle.

Carling gasped, her hand flying to her mouth as she looked over at Fyzzle. "Oh no! I'm so sorry Fyzzle."

The fisherman brushed off her concern with a wave of his hand. "Oh, don't you worry about me. I've been through much worse."

Overhearing the conversation, Kelfy ran up to check on his grandfather. "Grandpopi, are you hurt?" he asked. Tibbals, Tandum and Higson crowded around the old man as Pik repeated the story he'd told Carling.

"Carling, what would you like to do?" asked Tandum, deferring to her position as future queen.

"The way I see it," Carling said, "we need to get a good night's rest at the inn then set out for Duenton first thing in the morning."

"How will we get to the inn if the Heilodius are in Madiera searching for us?" asked Tibbals.

"I kin lead ye and make sure it be safe," offered Pik. "They be lookin' for a Faun with a red beard. I've completely fooled 'em, I have, thanks to Pernilla's skill with dyes and scissors," he said, chuckling while his hands fluffed up his short beard.

Carling mounted Tibbals and Higson mounted Tandum. Heavy flakes of snow began swirling around them as they headed for the trail that led them over a rocky ridge to Madiera. Soon the trail was slick with ice and snow. They made slow progress. Just as they reached the western edge of the fishing village, Pik stopped. "Carling and Higson, slide off the Centaurs. The Heilodius be expecting you to be ridin' 'em." The two Duende did as they were told.

Turning to Kelfy, Pik said, "Take yer grandfather back to yer shack and keep alert. I will take Carling and Higson first. Then I'll come back and get Tibbals and Tandum." Placing his hand on Carling's shoulder, he said, "Carling, stay behind me and back a way. Do what

I do. If I turn around, turn around as well. If I go down a side street, ye must also."

Carling nodded, feeling a wave of fear flow through her. "Got it," she whispered.

Kelfy took his grandfather's arm and guided him toward the wharf as Pik started walking into the village, keeping a careful lookout for the Heilodius Centaurs while working his way toward the inn. Carling waited just long enough to still be able to keep Pik in sight, then started walking. Higson followed after her, keeping his eyes glued to Carling's auburn curls as they bounced around between the snowflakes.

Numerous villagers and shoppers were still moving along the narrow, winding streets. Merchants were finishing up for the day and getting ready to close their doors. With a show of urgency, Pik motioned behind his back, pointing toward a shop that offered fishing equipment for sale. Carling stepped into the store and waited, peeking between the hanging nets and fishing poles. She didn't have to wait long. Soon, she spied two Heilodius Centaurs strolling past. They were noticeable in their typical black and silver shirts, though they had succumbed to the cold by wrapping winter scarves around their necks. Carling ducked, her heart pounding, hoping they weren't in the market for a new fishing pole.

"Can I help you with something?"

Carling sucked in her breath and jerked her head around. A Duende man, likely the shopkeeper, was standing a few feet away looking at her, his eyebrows raised, his head cocked to one side.

Slowly, Carling stood, glancing out the window in search of the Heilodius Centaurs as she did so. Turning back to the Duende, she said, "I'm trying to avoid someone."

The merchant smiled and nodded. "Ahh. I understand. A pretty girl like you probably has lots of boys chasing after her."

Carling felt her face turn red. She smiled. "Well, it isn't exactly like that. But thank you."

Just then Higson dashed into the store. "Oh, there you are."

The shopkeeper chuckled. "Just as I thought," he said with a knowing smile.

Higson looked back and forth between Carling and the shopkeeper.

"This is my friend," Carling said to the shopkeeper. "He's okay."

"Yes. Yes. Of course," he said, giving Carling a wink. "Well, you two have a wonderful day playing hide and seek. But I need to close up my shop now." He strode over to the door and opened it. Still smiling, he motioned outside with a sweep of his arm.

Carling and Higson walked cautiously to the door, peeking first one way then the other. There was no sign of the Heilodius Centaurs so they stepped out onto the cobblestone street. As they left the shop, Carling heard the merchant chuckle again and mumble, "Oh, to be young again."

CHAPTER 27

Back to the Inn

AS PIK KEPT WATCH at the end of the street, Carling and Higson hurried to the inn, weaving between the Duende, Ogres, and Cyclops that crowded the narrow street. Higson opened the door for Carling and she stepped inside, relief flowing through her. She felt safe at last. She wiped the nervous perspiration off her forehead and collapsed into an over-stuffed leather chair.

The innkeeper was sitting behind his desk, his little feet propped up on the front edge. When Carling entered, he lowered his feet and stood up. "Well, well, well. I see you have returned at last. I wondered if you had just left your Faun friend behind."

Carling let out the breath she had been holding while dashing through the village and shook the snowflakes out of her hair. She smiled at the innkeeper. "Yes. We are back from our journey."

"I'm glad to see that. Did you find what you were searching for?" he said, raising his eyebrows.

"Yes, we did."

Higson stepped up to the desk. "May we bother you for some rooms for the night?" he asked.

"Why, of course. That's why I'm here, you know. Will the Centaurs be joining you?"

"They should be here shortly," said Carling, glancing out the window.

"Would you like to stay right here by the warm fire and wait for them? That will give me time to ready your rooms," said the innkeeper with a smile that to Carling seemed contrived.

Carling felt a chill run through her and the Stone of Integrity grew warm. She forced her concern aside as she said, "We would like that very much, thank you." Then she took off her cape and shook off the snowflakes that were stubbornly clinging to it. Barely lifting her feet, she shuffled over to the fireplace and sat in a soft chair with a sigh. Higson sat in a little wooden chair beside her.

They didn't have to wait long for the Centaurs. With a whirl of winter wind and snow, Tibbals and Tandum, opened the door and hurried into the inn, their hooves clattering on the plank floor.

"My goodness," huffed Tibbals, "the weather is turning quite nasty. I'll bet my hair looks a fright!"

"Did you see the Heilodius Centaurs?" asked Carling.

"We saw them going into a tavern but they didn't see us," said Tandum, as he pulled his scarf from around his neck and fluffed his copper-colored hair. He swished his stubby tail and shook his horse-body to dislodge snowflakes.

The innkeeper served them a much-appreciated dinner of hot stew and biscuits, then showed them to their rooms. Carling was in the same room she'd occupied the last time they were there. Remembering the late-night visit by the innkeeper, she slid the old, rickety chair in front of the door. She set her cape on the seat of the chair and removed the Silver Breastplate, pausing long enough to finger the twinkling jewels. Too tired to undress further, the young Duende collapsed onto the bed, not even bothering to crawl under the covers, her shoes still snuggly tied to her dainty feet. Carling's eyes closed and she was soon in a deep, dreamless sleep.

Carling awoke with a start. Certain she'd heard something odd, she looked at the door. The chair was still where she'd left it, pressed tightly against the door with her cape draped across the seat.

Tap, tap.

Her pulse quickened, sending shivers racing through her body.

Tap, tap.

Slowly, Carling turned toward the window, from where it seemed the sound came. The snowstorm had dissipated, and she could see clouds racing one another back out to sea. A winter moon cast a cool, silver light into her room. From outside, a tiny hand appeared and rapped on the wavy glass.

Tap, tap.

Carling slid off the bed and tiptoed to the window. Her fingers reached up and turned the brass latch. She pushed open the window just a crack and peeked down. Standing below her window was the same waif who had taken her to see Hilgalda the Witch. Still dressed in rags, the pitiful little thing was shivering in the cold. Her large eyes were staring up at the window. When she saw Carling, she motioned with her hand. Carling could tell by the tenseness in her face that something was wrong and pushed opened the window further. A blast of cold air caused her to suck in her breath, but she leaned out the window anyway.

"Come with me. You're in danger," said the little Duende girl, her voice trembling.

Carling, her brow knitted in confusion, said, "What do you mean, I'm in danger?"

The witch's servant whimpered and looked from side to side. She turned back to Carling and said, "Hilgalda and the innkeeper have been waiting for your return. They are coming tonight to take you to the witch's hut."

"But why?"

"To capture you and hold you prisoner, I suppose. I don't really know. So, do you see why you must come with me?"

Just then, Carling heard the ominous creaking of floorboards outside her door. Her heart started pounding. She spun around and snatched the Silver Breastplate. Returning to the window, she shoved the breastplate out the window, letting it fall to the snow drift below, and crawled out behind it. As her feet touched the ground, she heard the hinges on her door creak and the legs of the chair scrape against the floor. Carling quickly pushed the window shut.

The little urchin started running toward the back of the building. Carling didn't follow. Instead, she peered through the window. With muscles quivering she watched as the light from a candle cast a yellow glow around the room, lighting the sneering faces of the innkeeper and the witch.

Carling gasped and jerked back, pressing her body against the rough, gray boards of the building. Her face turned ashen and her lips and chin trembled. "It's true then," she whispered.

"C-c-come. Come right n-now," hissed the little Duende girl between chattering teeth. She stood by the corner of the building and motioned frantically with her arms.

Carling bent down and grabbed the Silver Breastplate. She placed it on her body, latching it on the sides as she ran toward the waif.

"Now what?" asked Carling, feeling helpless and confused. She hadn't planned to be outside in the middle of a frigid winter night and knew she was not dressed warmly enough. As she considered the frightened eyes and ragged clothing of the little girl, she realized her helper wasn't any better off. Carling was sad that she didn't even have a cloak with her that she could wrap around the poor girl.

"I have a hiding place. Follow me." The waif turned on her dirty, shoeless heels and dashed away. This time, Carling followed.

CHAPTER 28

The Hiding Place

CARLING WAS SURPRISED BY how quickly the little Duende girl ran. As fast as she was, she was finding it difficult to keep up as the tiny thing scurried around corners and between buildings.

They were soon at the edge of the town, running down a rutted lane. Keeping her eyes focused on the retreating figure of the little girl, Carling kept moving as fast as she was able. They stayed along the lane as it wove through short, curling brush and trees. Her lungs stinging, Carling kept running along the narrow road as it climbed a hill. When they reached the top, Carling could just barely make out the gray, tilting shapes of headstones. The girl had brought her to a graveyard.

Here, the girl stopped. Pointing toward a cluster of headstones set to one side, she said, "Wait there. I will bring your friends to you when the sun rises."

Carling did as she was told and, peeking around the smallest stone, watched as the little girl disappeared back down the narrow lane. She turned around and sat on the ground, resting her back against the cold stone.

Now that Carling knew she would have to spend the rest of the night alone, the headstones around her became very frightening. Beads of cold sweat broke out on her forehead and she gulped down great breaths of air, trying to calm herself. The young Duende shivered, her teeth chattering from both the cold and fear. She wrapped her arms around her legs and rested her chin on her knees, trying to calm her pounding heart. Carling struggled to close her eyes and get some rest, but every sound made her jump, her eyes popping open. The crunch of dry leaves and the snap of a twig sounded like footsteps. The scratching of branches against the headstones sounded like grasping claws. The hoot of an owl sounded like a warning cry. She soon gave up any attempt to sleep.

After a long, bitterly cold night, filled with strange creaks and groans, the winter stars began to fade and the night sky lightened. Carling had never been more grateful for the arrival of a day than she was at that time. She stretched out her stiff legs and arms and stood up. In the gray light of a winter dawn, the headstones still seemed frightening.

Just before the sun rose over the Land Beyond on Crystonia's eastern border, Carling heard a familiar sound...the clip-clop of Centaur hooves. Holding her breath, she peeked around one of the headstones. With relief, she blew out her breath. Trotting toward her were Tandum and Tibbals. The little waif, her eyes wide, was riding on Tibbals's back, her arms tightly locked around the filly's waist.

Carling's relief and excitement were immediately replaced with fear and dread. Someone was missing. Tandum's back was empty. No Higson. "Where's Higson?" she shouted through the cold air, her breath sending out a puff of steam like a dragon.

"He's gone," Tibbals replied, bursting into tears.

"What?" said Carling, her words catching in her throat. "What do you mean, he's gone?"

The little urchin slid off Tibbals's back and ran up to her. "Oh, Miss Carling. Hilgalda and the innkeeper took him."

Carling shook her head in disbelief. "How do you know this?"

"When I got back to the inn, he was gone and so were they. His room was a mess."

Carling set her jaw as she thought about this new information. "Would they take him to Hilgalda's shack?"

The little girl nodded. "I think so. That's where Hilgalda likes to perform her magic."

CHAPTER 29

In the Shack

CARLING CLIMBED ON TIBBALS'S back as Tandum scooped up the little waif in his arms. "You're as light as a wisp of wind," he said with a quick smile. "I won't have any trouble carrying you in my arms."

The little girl giggled. If Carling could see beneath the smudges of dirt on the waif's face, she was sure that the little girl's cheeks were flushed. But Carling didn't take much time musing about it. Her eyes turned north, in the direction of Hilgalda's shack, her thoughts returning to Higson.

The two Centaurs galloped down the rutted road that led away from the graveyard. Struggling up the road, as fast as his two goat-legs would take him, was Pik. In his arms he carried Carling's bag.

Tibbals stopped in front of him. "Good job, Pik. Give Carling some clothing. She's freezing."

"No, don't bother," Carling said. "We don't have time. I'm fine. Give the little girl something, however. As for me, my only concern is finding Higson."

Though she was shivering and her teeth were chattering, she grabbed only her bow and quiver of arrows out of Pik's outstretched hands. "Thank you, Pik," she said as she clutched the few weapons she'd left at the inn with the Faun before her trip to Hy-Basilia. She turned back to face the northern shore. "Let's go."

The Centaurs picked up a rolling gallop again, causing Pik to throw his hands in the air and follow as best he could.

They skirted the edge of the village of Madiera and eventually reached the narrow, winding path that wove along the edge of the cliff. Below, the Swirling Sea bubbled and boiled, a gray monster threatening them and filling Carling with a sense of dread.

Ahead, Hilgalda's shack alternately disappeared and reappeared as bands of fog rolled in from the sea. The long, narrow row of steps leading up to the shack were partially covered with snow and completely covered with ice. Tiny Duende footprints were visible in the patches of snow.

Carefully placing their hooves, Tibbals and Tandum ascended the steps. They stopped at the top, a short distance from the cliff, over which the shack hung precariously, looking as though it were ready to fall into the Swirling Sea at any moment. A thin, gray tendril of smoke that twisted up into the sky from the stone chimney was quickly blown away by the wind coming off the sea. The goats bleated from their pen behind the shack. There were no other sounds and no other signs of life.

Carling slid off Tibbals's back. Hunched over, she tiptoed up to the shack. Pausing, the young Duende swallowed hard and set her jaw, her eyes locked on the crooked door with its peeling paint.

The little waif squirmed until Tandum bent over and lowered her to the ground. "Be careful, Miss Carling," she whispered. "Hilgalda will know you are here."

Carling averted her eyes from the door and looked down at the little girl. "I intend for her to," she said.

The girl whimpered and dashed toward the goat pen, disappearing behind the wall. Immediately, the goats stopped bleating.

Carling continued to move toward the front of the shack. As her foot touched the rough wood of the porch, a gust of wind blew her curls across her face and caught the rickety old door. It swung open with a loud bang. A figure shrouded in a cloak of shadows stepped out onto the rotting porch. Carling froze.

With a voice that sent shivers down Carling's spine, and caused goosebumps to rise on her skin, the figure said, "Why are you being so rude, coming to my home without an invitation? Well, since you are here, don't just stand there on my porch. Come in. I believe we have much to discuss." In a swirl of wind and mist, the witch disappeared.

The Stone of Integrity burned against Carling's chest from its place in the Silver Breastplate, which Carling wore unconcealed for everyone to see for the first time. She had made an important decision. No longer would she hide her calling. She would honor the responsibility she was given, and do so with confidence. Remembering the Wizard's words, "No longer hide who you are," Carling stepped toward the door of the witch's hut.

"Carling, wait!" Tibbals cried out.

"We're coming with you," said Tandum as he and his sister stepped onto the wooden porch, their hooves clopping loudly on the boards. Carling barely heard them, so focused was she now on finding Higson.

Carling peered around the doorframe. The interior of the shack was dark. No warm flames danced in the stone fireplace, only cooling, black cinders sending smoke curling up the chimney. Cobwebs formed shadows in all the corners and across the tops of windows. Even the spinning wheel sat deserted, its wheel creaking as it rocked forward and back, being pushed not by a foot but by the wind coming through the open door. Rats scurried back into the crevices, returning to their hiding places behind the walls.

Carling entered the room and instantly felt something brush against her legs. Jumping back, she looked down. Gazing up at her was the same large, yellow cat she had seen on her first visit to the shack. The cat meowed and purred as it wove between Carling's legs again. Out of habit more than affection, Carling bent down and stroked its long fur, her eyes still searching the gray corners of the room. The room was empty. Yet Carling had seen Hilgalda enter. At least she believed the shadowy figure who'd spoken to her had been the witch. But where had she gone?

The cat softly padded away a few feet, then stopped and looked back at Carling. It meowed, then walked a few steps farther before stopping and meowing again. "Do you want me to follow you?" whispered Carling.

The cat turned, its tail twitching, and walked past the deserted spinning wheel and the cold fireplace in the center of the room. Carling followed as silently as she was able, as did Tibbals and Tandum.

Behind the stone chimney, on the far wall of the shack, an old, darkened mirror in a tarnished frame appeared to be leaning against the wall. The cat walked up to it, looked back at Carling, then slipped behind it.

Carling hurried up to the mirror. It hung on hinges attached to the wooden wall on one side, leaving the other side free to swing open. Carling reached her hands around one side of the frame and pulled. The hinges creaked as the bottom edge of the frame scraped across the uneven wooden planks of the floor. Carling's mouth dropped open as she looked at what lay behind the mirror.

"It's a secret passageway," said Tibbals from behind her. "It appears to lead below the shack."

"It looks like a trap to me," added Tandum, clasping Carling's arm and pulling her back.

Carling looked back and forth from her friends to the tunnel. In the darkness, it was impossible to see how long the tunnel was, only that it angled down steeply. "Can you fit?" Carling asked her much taller companions.

"We'll duck," said Tibbals as she twisted her long hair into a bun and bent over. Tandum pursed his lips and let go of Carling's arm.

CHAPTER 30

Prisoner Beneath the Shack

CAUTIOUSLY, CARLING STEPPED THROUGH the doorway behind the mirror. She walked slowly forward, sliding her hand along a rough and slimy stone wall as she descended into the darkness. She felt cobwebs tickle her forehead and a spider wiggle down her cheek. A shiver went down her spine and she stifled a scream as she slapped the spider away.

She felt the ramp tilt at a steeper angle under her feet and struggled to keep from slipping. The air became thick and cold, and the hungry silence seemed to want to swallow her whole.

The ramp turned sharply to the left. Had she not been running her hand along the side of the tunnel, she would have run right into the stone wall where it rounded a corner. Turning to the left, Carling saw a faint light ahead. The rays of light wafted through the vibrating air, reflecting off the dust particles floating in the air and getting brighter as she moved closer. She felt something brush against her legs. She jumped and sucked in a quick breath...the orange cat. She let out a quiet sigh of relief and kept moving down the steep slope.

Stepping through an archway at the bottom of the ramp, Carling entered a brightly lit room. Beeswax candles set on candlesticks all around the room provided both light and a sweet aroma. Shelves filled with ancient, dusty books covered one wall. Bottles filled with colored liquids that looked like captured rainbows, lined another. Dried roots and flowers hung upside-down from strings stretched across the ceiling. The center of the room was dominated by a large table. Its legs were crooked and looked ready to collapse at any moment; the surface was smooth from years of polishing. The table top was covered with colanders as well as mortars and pestles of various sizes. A large, leather-bound book, its pages made from birch bark, lay on the table, open to one of its last pages. The room was a laboratory made for a witch.

Carling took in all of this in an instant. Suddenly, her eyes alighted on a cage in the darkness of a back corner. Inside the cage, curled up in a ball, was Higson.

Carling gasped and rushed forward. She clutched the metal bars of the cage and cried, "Higson! Higson! Are you alright?"

Higson lifted his eyes. They were bloodshot and puffy. His cheeks were flushed and blotchy. He slowly sat up. "Carling?" he said, his voice thick. "You found me." His eyes rolled back in his head and he collapsed back to the floor.

Tibbals and Tandum hurried up to the cage. "Oh no," Tibbals exclaimed, wiping a tear from her eye.

Tandum shook the cage. "Higson! Higson! Wake up!" he said, perspiration beading on his forehead.

"Welcome, my dear."

Carling, Tibbals, and Tandum whirled around to face Hilgalda the Witch. Standing beside her was the innkeeper.

"What have you done to Higson?" shouted Carling with a venom she had never known or tasted before.

"Tsk, tsk. Such a temper," Hilgalda said. "Very unbecoming of a queen."

Carling narrowed her eyes and blew out a long breath. "What. Have. You. Done. To. Higson?" she said, clipping off each word.

"Nothing permanent," the witch said. "Just quieted him down a little. I detest loud voices."

"Why did you take him?" Carling demanded, trying to keep her voice low.

"Why? To bring *you* here. You weren't where you were supposed to be when I came to get you. So, I borrowed your friend."

As the witch spoke, she floated like a shadow across the room until she was standing directly in front of Carling. "I took a chance that you liked him enough to come looking for him."

Carling lifted her chin in defiance. "What do you want from me?"

"Your stone, my dear. I need your stone," Hilgalda said, staring at the Silver Breastplate, with its three sparkling gems, covering Carling's clothing. "I have spent most of a lifetime trying to find the Stone of Integrity."

"For what purpose?" Carling asked as she covered the purple stone with her hand.

"Follow me and I will show you," said Hilgalda. With a graceful swish of the witch's hand, a tiny flaming torch appeared in the air. It floated like a butterfly in front of the witch as she scurried across the room, through the archway, and up the ramp. The light from the torch bounced along the cold, stone walls and cast fingers of shadows across the pathway. Though hesitant to leave Higson behind, Carling, Tibbals, and Tandum followed.

The witch led them through the doorway and back into the main room of the shack. She slid the mirror across the floor until all could see into it. Carling looked at the darkened glass. At first, she could see nothing unusual. Her violet eyes were staring back at her, her lips pressed together in concern. Behind her stood Tandum, his arms crossed over his chest and a frown on his face. Beside her stood Tibbals who was trying to fix an errant strand of hair. Then she noticed what was wrong. Hilgalda was not in the reflection.

Carling looked over at the witch, then back at the mirror. At the witch. Back at the mirror. Her chest tightened as she slowly shook her head. "I don't understand."

"It's quite simple, really. This mirror reflects only the true you."

"But...you are not there?"

"Exactly. The true Hilgalda has been lost for a very long time. I want her back."

Carling cocked her head. "I still don't understand what this has to do with me and the Stone of Integrity."

"The Stone of Integrity has great power...more than you will ever know," Hilgalda paused, then added, "...or need." She continued, "That stone has the power to bring back the real Hilgalda."

Tibbals placed a protective arm around Carling and gave her a gentle squeeze. Carling felt the Centaur's love flow into her. "Hilgalda," Carling said, "I greatly desire to help you, but I can't give you the Stone of Integrity. It isn't mine to give. It belongs to the Silver Breastplate."

Hilgalda's face darkened and her sharp, green eyes became cold and hard. She glared at Carling with open hatred. "You won't give it to me, you say?"

"It isn't that I *won't*," Carling said, heart aching for the pain she saw in Hilgalda's eyes, "I simply can't."

"Then you will never see your friend again!" In a flash, Hilgalda disappeared and the mirror slammed shut, causing the little shack to tremble.

"Hilgalda!" cried Carling.

Tandum dashed for the mirror. With all his strength, he pried open the mirror and grunted as he held it open, his muscles bulging from the strain. Carling and Tibbals hurried through the narrow opening. As soon as they were past, Tandum stepped around the mirror and onto the ramp just as it slammed shut behind him.

Carling led the way down the ramp. Tibbals and Tandum followed, their hooves pounding on the slanted boards. Carling held her hands out in front of her to keep from running into the wall she knew was somewhere ahead. As soon as the palms of her hands rammed into the wall, she turned left. The dim lights ahead pulled her forward with a power of their own.

Gasping for breath, Carling entered the underground laboratory where she slid to a stop. Higson was spread out on the table in the center of the room, which had been cleared of everything it had held earlier. He wasn't moving. His eyes were half-closed, his mouth gaping open. Hilgalda stood beside Higson. The innkeeper stood over him, holding a silver knife suspended above his heart. Carling's eyes widened, and her jaw dropped. Her stomach clenched so tightly she felt like she was being pinched in half.

Tibbals and Tandum rushed into the room behind her. Carling stretched out her arms to stop them. At the sight of their friend in such danger, Tibbals let out a startled scream and Tandum growled like a lion.

"Hilgalda," Carling said, trying to keep her voice calm while hiding her quivering hands behind her back. She tried desperately to control the panic building inside and appear self-assured. "Why are you doing this?"

"I want you to understand the pain I have been suffering," the witch said.

"But Higson has nothing to do with any of this."

"Maybe not. But his loss would bring *you* pain." The witch floated up to Carling like a gust of wind, facing her with a look of pure evil. "I will make a trade...the boy for the stone."

Carling shook her head in disbelief as Tandum bolted forward, stopped only by Tibbals as she clutched his arm. "Wait, Tandum," his sister whispered, her eyes locked on the innkeeper still poised over Higson's prone body.

The big yellow cat, who had been lolling on a shelf much too small for her, opened her golden eyes and stood on her four large paws. Suddenly, the cat let out a low growl that sounded more like a tiger's than a cat's. She snarled and, in one swift movement, leaped across the room and landed on the innkeeper's outstretched arm, her claws digging into his skin. The innkeeper cried out in pain and dropped the knife. Carling watched it glance off the edge of the table and onto the floor, spinning toward her.

Carling bolted forward and reached for the knife. As her fingers folded around the wooden handle, footsteps sounded from above...an army of footsteps. Carling heard the mirror scraping across the floorboards, then stomping feet moving down the ramp as dancing flames lit the tunnel, sending bouncing shadows into the laboratory.

"Kill the Witch! Kill the Witch!" The shouts echoed down the stone walls, sending chills through Carling. The knife still in her hand, she turned to face the archway and the army coming toward them.

"Kill the Witch! Kill the Witch!" The shouting was so loud, the shack above was shaking and the bottles in the laboratory were rattling.

Time seemed to stand still. The sound of her breathing echoed in Carling's head as the sound of the stomping footsteps echoed through her body. Carling bit her lip and straightened up as tall as she was able. She held up both hands and waited for the mob to enter the laboratory.

Pik was in the lead, followed by a dozen fishermen from the village. "Kill the...!" As soon as he saw Carling, Pik ran toward her. "Carling! Carling! Be ye alright, Missy?"

"Stop right there, Pik...all of you...stop," said Carling, her voice low but firm.

Pik slid to a stop, his mouth open, his gray and black beard resting on his chest.

All became silent.

The shadows stopped moving. The feet stopped marching. Even the flecks of dust stopped floating in the air. No one said a word.

All eyes were on Carling as though no one knew just what she was going to do next. The knife, still in her hand, glinted in the orange light cast by the torches.

The first sound was from the cat. It released a deep, threatening growl as it let go of the innkeeper's arm and leapt to the floor. The cat padded noisily over to Carling and rubbed against her leg.

"Pik," Carling said, "no one is going to kill anyone. Hilgalda just needs help."

"It not be the witch that needs help, Carling," Pik said. "She kidnapped Higson, didn't she? I be afraid she captured you as well, so I recruited some help. It wasn't hard to get people to come with me. Apparently, lots o' people in the village have a bone ta pick with Hilgalda."

"I'm sure that's true, Carling said, "but killing her, or even threatening her, is not the answer." Carling looked past Pik and addressed the fishermen. "I truly appreciate your concern for me but, as you can see, I am fine. You may go back to your boats and shops. I can take care of things here."

At first no one moved. Then Carling heard grumbling from the crowd.

"She doesn't know what she is saying."

"The witch has her under a spell!"

"But look what she's wearing."

"It looks like a silver breastplate."

"Could it be *the* Silver Breastplate? The one we have been waiting so long for?"

"What? Who said 'the Silver Breastplate?'"

"I did. Look what she's wearing."

"Move out of the way," said a particularly short Duende as he pushed to the front. "I want to see for myself."

He came to an abrupt stop. "Oh, my," said the Duende, the owner of the town's mercantile. "Have you ever seen jewels so lustrous or silver so pure?"

"Settle ye down everyone," said Pik, blocking them with outstretched arms. "Yes, it be *the* Silver Breastplate. Carling be preparing to be our new queen."

"Our new queen?"

"Really?"

"Did he say our new queen?"

"That's what he said."

The short Duende who had worked his way to the front slowly lowered himself to one knee and bowed his head. "Your Majesty," he said reverently.

One by one, all the fishermen lowered themselves and bowed their heads.

Seeing them kneeling before her made Carling feel very uncomfortable. "Please stand. You do not need to bow to me."

With a screech, Hilgalda whirled to the front of the laboratory. She stopped in front of Carling, her hands on her hips. "What do you mean when you say you will help me?" she demanded. "How can you help me if you won't give me the Stone of Integrity?"

"As I said," Carling answered, relieved to see the fishermen returning to their feet. "I can't give you the

stone as it belongs to the Silver Breastplate. But,"
Carling paused, her heart pounding out a nervous
rhythm, "I believe if you will but touch the stone, its
power will bring back the true Hilgalda."

The witch stiffened, eyeing Carling with suspicion.
Slowly, she stretched forth one hand. Even more slowly,
she stepped forward. Carling waited, desperately
hoping this would work.

Hilgalda hesitated just before her hand reached the
stone.

The hunger in the witch's eyes terrified Carling, but
there was a sadness there as well. It was the sadness
that motivated Carling as the Stone of Mercy warmed
her chest. She took a slow breath, quelling her fear. "Go
ahead," she whispered. "Bring back the true Hilgalda."

Hilgalda cautiously took one more step forward,
reached out her crooked finger, and touched the purple
Stone of Integrity. Carling felt a charge of energy flow
through her body and saw a flash of purple light shoot
out from the Silver Breastplate and straight toward the
witch. A stream of purple stars created a web of
sparkling light that engulfed Hilgalda. The sea of stars
swirled around the laboratory, taking Hilgalda with
them, swooshed under the archway, forcing the
fishermen to duck their heads, and carried the witch up
the ramp.

The stunned fishermen stepped out of Carling's way
as she made a dash past them and up the ramp,
following the stream of stars. When she reached the
top, she entered the main room of the witch's shack.
The room was glowing with a purple light that sent
rainbow shadows around the room and lit every nook
and cranny.

Carling stepped around to the front of the mirror where the web of swirling stars began to fold and pucker, twist and turn, until it congealed into the form of a beautiful, young Duende woman. Radiating with a purple light, the woman stood before the mirror and smiled at her reflection. She slowly turned to face Carling. "Thank you, my Queen," she said.

CHAPTER 31

The New Hilgalda

CARLING GASPED AND STEPPED back. "Who...who are you?" she stammered.

With the elegance of a swan, the woman stepped closer. The green eyes melting into Carling could only belong to one person...Hilgalda. They were the same eyes without the hunger. But this was not the same Hilgalda. Instead of the gnarled, old woman bent over with age and arthritis, the woman standing in front of her was young and beautiful. Her skin, rather than gray, had a pearlescent glow Carling had never seen before. Her body was tall for a Duende, though not as tall as Carling's, and straight. Her hair was no longer thin and white. It draped around her shoulders in thick ringlets the color of rich mahogany. Her rags had been replaced by a flowing purple gown that rippled like a cascading waterfall.

Carling pressed her hands to her cheeks and shook her head. "Hilgalda? How did this happen?"

"*You* did it, my dear Queen. It was all you. You showed mercy to me, even when I didn't deserve it. You had the courage to try to help me, even when you were frightened. And you shared with me the power of the Stone of Integrity so I might escape the curse of deceit placed upon me centuries ago."

Carling was not aware that Tibbals and Tandum, having followed her up the ramp, were standing right behind her until Tibbals inhaled sharply. "Who is this?" she asked.

Carling, running her hands through her auburn curls, turned to face them. Her head shaking in disbelief, she said, "It's Hilgalda."

"Hilgalda?" said Tibbals, her eyes wide as she extended her hand as though she wanted to touch this apparition.

"Not possible," said Tandum, his brows knotting together.

Carling spun back around to face Hilgalda. "If you *are* Hilgalda as you say, you must correct a grievous sin." Pointing toward the tunnel, Carling said. "My dear friend, Higson, needs to be healed of whatever it is you did to him. And you need to do it right now!"

"Oh, dear," Hilgalda said, "The poor boy. I'll take care of that this instant."

Hilgalda glided elegantly past Carling and back down the ramp, Carling, Tibbals, and Tandum on her heels. The fishermen hadn't moved, looks of fear and disbelief, coupled with confusion, still on their faces. When the beautiful creature that Hilgalda had become appeared on the ramp, their eyes opened wide with admiration, giving them a new reason not to move. She flowed past like a breath of spring, paying no attention to them.

Back in the cellar, Hilgalda approached the table in the middle of the laboratory. While the innkeeper was now huddled in a corner, nursing his injured arm, the orange cat was sitting atop Higson's prone body, sending threatening glares at the innkeeper.

"You may go," Hilgalda said to the innkeeper with a dismissive wave. "I'll take care of this, now."

The innkeeper slowly stood, his eyes wide with shock, his mouth twisted with confusion. He stepped backwards until his back pressed against the cold, stone walls of the cellar. The fishermen, sensing that the chores awaiting them were more important than watching the actions of a reformed witch, retreated up the ramp. Carling hurried forward and stood beside Higson. She watched Hilgalda, anxious to see Higson well again. The cat stayed where she was, looked up at Carling, and purred loudly.

"Let me see...let me see," Hilgalda murmured. She floated across the room to where the old, leather-bound book Carling had seen earlier, sat askew on top of a cabinet. The witch pulled it down, opened the cover, and carefully turned each birch-bark page, running her finger down each page as she mumbled to herself. "No, not that. No, that won't do. Now, where is it? I know it's in here somewhere."

Page after page brought the same result, even to the very last. "I must have missed it," Hilgalda said over her shoulder. "Let me look again."

The witch repeated the process, turning and examining each page. Nothing.

Hilgalda straightened and turned toward Carling, a frown on her beautiful face that did nothing to detract from her beauty. "I think I may have been a little too enthusiastic when I gave him that drought."

Carling felt her heart start to pound as she clutched her hands into fists, feeling her nails digging into her palm. She narrowed her eyes. "What do you mean?" she said, trying to keep her voice calm.

"I can't remember everything I gave him," said Hilgalda, her face blushing like a young girl.

"Are you trying to tell us," said Tandum between clenched teeth, "that you don't know how to cure him?"

"Maybe if I had a little more time...maybe then I could remember."

Carling glared at Hilgalda, the sweet scent of the beeswax candles suddenly making her feel sick. "How much time?" she asked.

Hilgalda shrugged.

"This is my best friend's life we're talking about," Carling said. "So, I ask again, 'How much time?'"

Hilgalda shook her head, her eyes beseeching Carling for understanding. "I don't know. I've never done this type of spell before."

"Well, try *something*," suggested Tibbals.

"Yes. Yes. Let me try something." Hilgalda turned and grabbed bottles of various sizes filled with rainbow-colored liquid from the shelf. She snatched some herbs from the ceiling and crushed them in her fist, letting them fall into a stone bowl. To these, she added drops of liquid from the jars. A sizzling sound erupted, and steam floated to the ceiling. She took a small ladle and scooped some of the concoction into a metal cup. Floating over to Higson, she lifted his head and poured some of the sizzling liquid down his throat.

Higson coughed and gagged, causing the cat to leap off his chest with a screech. Higson's eyes flew open and his body began jerking around in spasms. Carling gasped and reached out for him as Tandum rushed over and supported him so he wouldn't fall over the edge. When the jerking stopped, Higson slumped back, his tongue dangling from the side of his mouth.

"Oh, no!" moaned Carling. "What have you done?"

Tibbals stepped forward. "I think we need to send for Pernilla Persdotter."

Tandum and Pik immediately dashed off to find the healer. Carling remained standing beside Higson. Her heart was aching with worry as she looked down at her friend, barely able to see him through the tears that filled her eyes. His hand, which she clutched tightly, felt damp and cold. He was breathing through his gaping mouth, but his breaths were shallow and his eyes remained rolled back in his head. He didn't respond when Carling talked to him. He didn't even respond when she bent over, hugged him, and kissed his sunken cheek.

Occasionally, Carling glanced at Hilgalda, who continued to search through her old book. Then she looked toward the archway that led to the ramp, willing Tandum and Pik to appear with Pernilla Persdotter. She watched Tibbals pace back and forth across the dirt floor of the cellar. At last, she heard hoofbeats on the floor above. The young Duende ran up the ramp, meeting Tandum and Pernilla on their way down. Both the Centaur and the healer had their arms full of bottles and bags of dried herbs. Pik came down the ramp last, huffing and puffing, having had a difficult time keeping up with Tandum. In his arms, he carried Pernilla's mortar and pestle.

Pernilla Persdotter hurried over to Higson, setting her bottles down on the table near his head. "Shoo, shoo," she said, waving her hand at the cat, sending the furry creature scurrying across the room yowling. The cat leaped up to a shelf where she planted herself, a look of irritation on her whiskered face. She remained there and watched, her gold eyes moving from one creature to another, then back to Higson.

The famous Duende healer examined Higson, checking his breathing and heartbeat. She brushed back his wavy, brown hair and placed her cheek against his forehead. She held his hands in hers, massaging his palms with her thumbs, her eyes narrowed in thought. Next, she turned her attention to his feet. She removed his leather shoes and rubbed his feet and legs, humming to herself and gazing off into the air above everyone's heads.

No one in the room moved. Even Hilgalda stopped searching for a cure and stood near the table watching the healer at work.

Pernilla Persdotter lifted one dainty finger and winked an eye. "I know just what we need," she said, spinning around and grabbing bottle after bottle, opening lids, and shaking drops into a bowl. The liquid became a swirl of pink and purple and let off a twisting ribbon of pale blue smoke. She grabbed the mortar and pestle from Pik and crushed several herbs into the bowl. With the pestle, she pounded and ground the leaves and flower petals until they were as fine as dust.

These she stirred into the steaming, pastel liquid, turning it a disgusting shade of green. It reminded Carling of the split-pea soup her mother made, a soup she'd detested. The smell was much different, however. This concoction smelled like the outhouse behind her family's cottage in Duenton when it needed to be cleaned. She sincerely hoped Pernilla was not going to feed this to Higson.

Pernilla placed the mixture over a candle. The ingredients immediately began to boil and foam, sending a green stream of bubbles up and over the side of the bowl. Pernilla caught the foam in her hand and rushed over to Higson. She rubbed the bubbles over his face, avoiding his sagging mouth and drooping eyes. She rushed back to the bowl and gathered more foam. This she held in one hand. With the other, she pulled open the laces that held Higson's shirt closed and spread the shirt open, exposing his chest. Rubbing both hands together until they were coated with the green bubbles, she spread the foam over his torso.

Higson began to cough...at first softly but then violently. Carling, fear overtaking her, clenched her hands into tight fists and pressed her lips into a narrow line. She kept her eyes glued on Higson.

Groaning and clasping his stomach, Higson slowly opened his eyes. "Oh-h-h, I don't feel so good."

Carling dashed up to him and threw her arms around him, laughing with relief. "Higson, Higson. You're back!"

CHAPTER 32

Judging the Guilty

FOOTSTEPS SOUNDED OVERHEAD. SOON the little waif, followed by Kelfy, entered the cellar.

"Carling!" said Kelfy as he pulled her back from Higson and wrapped his arms around her. "Are you alright? The fishermen told me you were here."

Higson moaned again causing Carling to push Kelfy away and turn back to her old friend. "What do you need, Higson?" she said, her brow wrinkled.

"Just you," he said.

Kelfy looked toward the ceiling and gave a soft snort.

"Well," said Pernilla Persdotter, the smile on her face showing how pleased she was with herself, "I can see I am no longer needed here. I'll just be on my way."

"Let Lilara walk you to the door," offered Hilgalda, giving the waif a gentle smile. "You don't mind, do you my dear?"

The little Duende girl stared up at Hilgalda, her face lined with fear as well as shock. "Who? Who..." she stuttered.

Hilgalda laughed with delight.

"Lilara?" exclaimed Tibbals. "What a lovely name. It reminds me of 'lily.' Let me take Lilara to the inn and get her looking as beautiful as a flower."

Tibbals took the child by the hand and, followed by Pernilla, disappeared up the ramp.

"Ye wait fer me," shouted Pik. "I'll go with ye to make sure ye be safe." Pik's cloven hooves clicked as he ran up the ramp.

The innkeeper slunk down and attempted to follow them.

"Wait just a minute," said Carling stepping away from Higson to block the archway. "You have a punishment coming."

Rubbing his hand through his hair and gulping loudly the innkeeper stopped where he was and begin fidgeting, hopping from one foot to the other. He dropped his chin to his chest. Pointing to Hilgalda, he mumbled, "It was her fault. She made me do it."

"No one can *make* anyone do anything," Carling said. "You chose to do what you did. Now you both must pay for your crimes."

Hilgalda nodded and stepped forward. "Any punishment will be worth paying, so grateful am I to have my true self back.

The innkeeper snapped his head around and glared at the witch. "That's easy for *you* to say," said the innkeeper, "but what do *I* get out of this? Only trouble as far as I can see."

"That's the result of making bad choices, and following the wrong people," said Tandum, pressing his fists against his hips.

"Hilgalda," said Carling.

Hilgalda set down the small hand mirror she was gazing into. She smiled. "Yes, Your Majesty?"

"The punishment I am going to give you is actually a privilege in disguise," Carling said. "You and the innkeeper will be responsible for Lilara. From this day, forward, that little girl will be under your care...and it will be a care filled with kindness. She is to be well fed, clothed and educated. She will have the finest room in the inn for her home."

"Is that it? Is that our punishment?" asked Hilgalda.

"That is it," said Carling, her eyes soft, her mouth forming a gentle smile.

"Thank you, Your Majesty," Hilgalda said, bowing. "We will do as you command." She nudged the innkeeper with her elbow.

"Yes, Your Majesty. We will do exactly as you have commanded," he said, sounding almost giddy. "Only the best for our little Lilara."

CHAPTER 33

The Graveyard

WORD OF THE APPEARANCE of the Silver Breastplate on a young Duende girl spread through the little fishing village. By the time Carling left the witch's shack with Kelfy beside her and Higson in Tandum's arms, a large crowd of villagers...men, women, and children...were waiting at the bottom of the long stairway. They were standing in the snow and shivering, but their eyes sparkled with anticipation of seeing a queen. A loud cheer arose when they saw Carling wearing the Silver Breastplate.

"There she is. There's our queen," shouted one woman.

"It's true. The Silver Breastplate has been given to a Duende," exclaimed another.

Carling's cheeks flushed red but not from the cold. Being the center of so much attention and adulation was going to take some getting used to. Carling waved and smiled and then ducked her head, looking down at the snow-covered ground so as not to show her embarrassment. Kelfy draped his own cape over her shoulders, covering the breastplate and providing much needed warmth on the cold, winter day.

Gray, swirling clouds filled the sky, and the wind tossed the sea foam over the small group as they descended the stairs. A gauzy sea mist floated around Carling's shoulders like a ghostly veil, adding to the aura of mystique that surrounded her as the foretold wearer of the Silver Breastplate.

But beneath that aura, Carling was just like anyone else standing or moving about on that winter day. Her teeth chattered and she shuddered against the cold as she stepped daintily through the snow. The crowd parted only slightly to allow her to pass, hands reaching out to touch the cloak she wore as it fluttered in the wind.

Not everyone in the village of Madiera was celebrating the appearance of the wearer of the Silver Breastplate, however. The Heilodius Centaurs who had been searching for Carling for several weeks, were holed up in an abandoned cabin on the south side of the village. Peering through a crack in the boarded-up windows, one of their number noticed the Duende of the village rushing through the streets, heading in the direction of the witch's shack.

"What's going on out there?" he asked his companions.

"Maybe someone caught the sea monster they're always talking about," said one with a sneer.

The others laughed.

"No, really. Something has the whole village riled up. I'm going out to see what's happening," said the Centaur who had spoken first.

"Be my guest. I'm staying in by the fire," said the leader known as Reemer, Zarius's right-hoof man. Zarius, the leader of the Heilodius Centaurs, was determined to stop Carling in her quest to complete the Silver Breastplate and inherit the throne.

All the others in the cabin happily followed Reemer's example and stayed where they were, lounging around the fireplace, but the Centaur who had voiced his concern threw a cloak over his shoulders and went out the door. The cold wind blasted him in the face, and he pulled the collar of the cloak up until only his eyes were visible. For a moment, he had second thoughts...sitting by the fire suddenly sounded very nice. But for this Centaur, curiosity overpowered comfort. He left the crumbling cottage and followed the Duende as the little people dashed toward Hilgalda's shack.

When the crowd came to a stop at the base of the cliff upon which Hilgalda's shack hung precariously above the Swirling Sea, the Centaur hid behind a clump of wind-swept pine trees. He watched and waited, listening to the crowd talking about the Silver Breastplate. He smiled. *This is it! I've found her. Zarius will make me a hero.* A sardonic grin split his face and he rubbed his freezing hands together in glee.

A cheer from the crowd interrupted his self-praise, and the Centaur looked up toward the shack from which a beautiful, auburn-haired Duende girl was now exiting. Compared to the other Duende, she was quite tall. But it was neither her height nor her beauty that caught the Centaur's attention. Over her torso, she wore a silver breastplate. The Centaur watched as another Duende covered her and the breastplate with a cape and she descended the pathway. He continued watching as the crowd called out to her and pushed around her, attempting to touch her. As the girl reached the cobblestone road that led along the shore and into town, the Centaur spun around and started cantering back to tell Reemer and the others what he'd seen.

Higson felt weak but secure with Tandum carrying him. As they walked down the stone steps, he opened his eyes only slightly. Peeking through his eyelashes, he watched Carling and Kelfy move through the crowd of excited villagers. His body grew tense and he gritted his teeth when he saw Kelfy wrap his arm around Carling's waist and guide her down the hill.

Just as Tandum's hooves touched the icy cobblestones of the village streets, the Centaur slipped, his legs flaying out in all directions. Higson's eyes flew open and he started as Tandum struggled to stay upright.

When the Centaur steadied himself, Higson looked ahead and noticed the retreating form of another Centaur. He knew from the attire that it was one of the Heilodius Centaurs Pik warned them about. His heart pounding, he watched the Centaur disappear up a narrow side street.

"Tandum, look there," he said, too weak to point. "Look up that street."

Tandum turned his head. "A Centaur. Yes, I see him."

"Do you suppose...?"

"A Heilodius?" Tandum interrupted. "It must be. Look what he's wearing. Let's get to the inn quickly."

Back at the inn, Tibbals was delighted with the transformation she was creating with the little Duende named Lilara. The filly was completely in her element. She'd filled a metal tub with warm water and bubbles so Lilara could bathe. She'd curled the little girl's hair with ribbons and dressed her in one of her own pink blouses. On Lilara the blouse became a dress, the bottom edge resting on the tops of the Duende's tiny feet.

The young girl no longer looked like a street urchin and couldn't seem to contain her joy. Her eyes danced and she smiled broadly, waving at everyone as they came into the room.

"Oh, Lilara," Carling gushed as she entered the inn with Kelfy and spotted the transformed child. "You look so beautiful."

Lilara twirled around, holding out her dress. "Tibbals did it," she said as tears filled her eyes and threatened to spill onto her cheeks.

Tibbals glowed with pride as she looked down at her little protégé.

The celebration was short lived, however. As soon as Tandum and Higson entered the inn, they shared what they had seen on their way through the village.

"A Centaur was watching the crowd when Carling walked through the village," said Tandum, setting Higson down on a soft chair and shaking out his tired arms. "Higson and I are sure it was a member of the Heilodius Herd. He was wearing a black shirt."

Carling's head jerked up. "Did he see me?"

"We think so," said Tandum. "How could he miss you? Everyone was looking at you and talking about the Silver Breastplate."

"Do you think they saw you come to the inn?" asked Tibbals.

"I don't know. But they very well could have," answered Tandum.

Pik stepped forward. "We need to get ye out o' here, Missy," he said to Carling. "We need to get all of us out o' here," he added.

"I think we need to start back to Duenton," said Higson, his voice weak.

"To Duenton?" said Tibbals. "In this weather? And Higson...you are in no condition to travel."

"Higson is right. It's too risky to stay here," agreed Tandum as he scratched his chin and scowled. "I can help Higson. We need to pack up and leave the inn immediately, one at a time so as not to attract any attention."

"That's a good idea," said Kelfy. "But if we go one at a time, where should we go and where should we meet?"

Higson glared at Kelfy. "What do you mean by *we*?"

"Didn't Carling tell you?" asked Kelfy with a cock of his head and a smirk on his face. "But then again, why would she confide in you? In any case, I'm coming with you...at least as far as Duenton. I think all of you could use my help."

Higson pressed his lips tightly together and turned away. He said nothing more.

Lilara bounced to the middle of the room. "I know. I know where we can meet," she said.

All eyes turned to the little Duende. "Where, Lilara?" asked Tibbals.

"In the old graveyard. I could lead you there one at a time. No one ever goes there...except me."

Not that horrible graveyard again, thought Carling, but she said nothing.

It was agreed that Carling would go first out of fear that the Heilodius Centaurs knew where she was and might be coming for her soon. The rest would gather supplies for the journey and go to the graveyard one at a time.

The snow was falling again so the future Queen of Crystonia placed a wool cloak over her shoulders, covered her head with the hood, and tied a scarf around her neck. She grabbed what few items she had and went to the door. Pik went outside first to see if the Heilodius Centaurs were around. He came back a short time later, snowflakes sticking to his forelock, dangling ears and curling horns, to say that all was clear...no sign of the Heilodius.

Lilara, wrapped in a cloak that was much too big for her, led Carling out the door, around the corner of the inn and through narrow, curving alleyways that few traveled, even on the most pleasant days. By the time they reached the edge of the village, the snow had stopped and a narrow shaft of golden sunlight slid sideways from the west across the white landscape, a final farewell to the day.

Carling and Lilara followed a narrow path that wound over sand dunes and up to the graveyard. Lilara didn't seem the least bit frightened as she squeezed between the rusted bars of an iron fence and stepped into the burial ground. Carling followed, not feeling quite so comfortable, remembering the first night she spent alone with the crumbling tombstones.

Most of the grave markers were old stones that looked horribly like hunched over Duende covered in gray robes. Any inscriptions on the stones had long since been worn away by wind and sea spray. On the far side of the graveyard were four equally old stone tombs that looked like little houses. Each was built with a low, arched doorway that opened into absolute darkness. Carling did not remember seeing these the first time she was in the graveyard. It was into one of these that Lilara directed Carling.

"Wait right here. I'll go get the others. It shouldn't be long," said Lilara. The little Duende girl spun around and disappeared into the gathering darkness.

Carling slid to the ground and threw her cloak over her knees. She tilted her head back and rested it against the stone wall of the tomb. Her eyes adjusted slowly to the darkness. Eventually she could just make out the inscriptions on the tombs in front of her.

Simpston – The Greatest of All Fishermen
Marbalina – A Victim of the Adaro
Chesterny – Mayor of Madiera

Carling's mind began conjuring images of the Duende who were buried here, and she tried to imagine what their lives had been like...especially Marbalina's. What did the Adaro do to her? Thinking about the Duende whose names were on the gravestones kept Carling occupied for quite a while. Eventually, however, her thoughts drifted back to the present and she realized that it was completely dark outside the tomb. Clearly, it was well into the night. She wondered why Lilara was not yet back with the others. She shivered at the thought of spending the night alone in this tomb.

Suddenly something brushed against her legs. "E-e-e-k! Help!" she shouted. Too frightened to get up and run, she dared only look down. Her heart nearly burst with relief. What rubbed against her was only a cat. The creature turned back and rubbed against her again, purring. It stopped and looked up at Carling, its golden eyes making her think that it knew secrets it would not tell.

"Oh, you frightened me," said Carling. "But don't go. I am truly glad for your company."

A large, silver moon peeked out behind breaks in scuttling clouds, sending a beam of white light directly into the tomb. In the light, Carling could see the cat more clearly. It was Hilgalda's big yellow cat, the same cat that had followed them through the village, the same cat that had saved Higson from the innkeeper's knife. Carling wondered how the cat always seemed to be close by.

Carling stretched forth her hand and stroked the long yellow fur. "It's you. I'm so glad. I didn't get a chance to thank you properly for saving my friend."

The cat dipped its head in a bow and turned in a graceful circle.

Carling giggled. "You understand every word I say, don't you?"

The cat let out a pleasant meow and curled up on top of Carling's frozen feet.

"Thank you, dear friend. That keeps my toes warm," said Carling. "Do you know what has become of my friends? I thought they would be here by now."

The cat meowed again, tucked its head between its paws, and closed its large eyes. It immediately began purring, the rumbling shaking its whole body.

Carling smiled down at her welcome company. She didn't like the thought of spending the night alone among the frightening tombs and headstones. Even worse were the possible reasons she conjured for the delay of her friends. They were supposed to meet at the graveyard. Why weren't they here? Where were they? Had something terrible happened? Had the Heilodius captured them?

Time, measured by the movement of the moon peeking behind the veil of clouds, moved slowly. Carling drifted off to sleep, though even in her dreams she continued wondering what had happened to Higson, Tibbals, Tandum, Pik, and Kelfy.

Carling was awakened by an unfamiliar noise. She lay quite still, barely opening her eyes; she was quite sure she would be even more frightened if she saw what had made the sound. The cat stood and hissed, curling its lips back to reveal a set of wicked-looking teeth. It arched its back, its hair standing on end, and thrust its puffy tail straight up into the air. Its yellow eyes were glued on the darkness outside the tomb.

Carling waited to see if the sound would return. She didn't have to wait long. When the noise came again, it was louder...a harsh, piecing howl from somewhere among the tombstones. Carling opened both eyes wide and sat up.

By now, the clouds had been pushed out to sea by the wind and the moon was shining brightly, casting wiggling shadows from the tombstones across the snow-covered ground. The cry came again...louder and closer. Carling saw something race between two lopsided stones. The cat screeched and dashed out the arched doorway, disappearing into the night. Carling wished it hadn't left. She felt very alone...and very frightened. Her heart pounded wildly beneath the Silver Breastplate and droplets of cold sweat broke out on her forehead.

Carling forced herself to stand. Just as she did so, a golden jackal stepped across the opening of the tomb, stopped and turned to face her. Carling watched, her body rigid, not even breathing.

The jackal was the size of a large dog. His body was lean and covered with coarse, golden fur. His small, eyes...eyes that were presently locked on her...flashed with red.

Carling shifted her eyes as she looked for a place to hide. On both sides of her, the walls of the tomb were smooth all the way to the ceiling. Slowly, she slid her hands behind her back, her fingers searching for any sort of escape, only to find that the wall behind her was as smooth and solid as the others. The only way out of the tomb was through the archway...the one under which the jackal stood.

The jackal neither moved nor made a sound.

Carling felt the Stone of Courage grow warm against her chest. She locked her eyes on the jackal's eyes and noticed that they seemed to be filled with curiosity more than hunger. Gradually, cautiously, she brought one hand up to her throat and unlatched her cape. It fell to the floor, landing in a pile around her feet. The Silver Breastplate glowed with light, filling the darkness of the tomb. The jackal's eyes registered surprise, and he took one step back before stopping again.

Trapped between intrigue and terror, Carling stood her ground, wondering how long this standoff would last before the wild animal attacked...if he was even going to.

The jackal cocked his head to one side and his eyes changed to a more natural black before he lowered his eyelids. He dropped his head and stepped forward, dragging his long claws across the stone surface of the tomb. When he was just a Centaur's tail-length away from Carling, he stopped and lowered his body to the ground, placing his muzzle on his front paws and closing his eyes.

CHAPTER 34

Duplicity

AS SOON AS LILARA left Carling alone in the tomb, the waif ran as quickly as her little legs could take her back to the village. She squeezed between close-set buildings and houses and around trees and bushes. The little Duende kept herself as hidden as possible as she worked her way back to the inn. Just as she came around a corner that brought the back of the inn to view, she jerked to a stop. Crouched to the side of the building, peeking around to the front, were two large Centaurs, black capes covering their human torsos and extending over their equine bodies clear to their tails. Scarfs were wrapped around their faces. Even with the added clothing, Lilara had no trouble recognizing who they were. They were silently watching and waiting...Lilara was sure she could guess for what.

She circled around the neighboring building, a shop that sold household goods to the town's Duende, and walked up the boardwalk right toward the inn. She was only partially confident that they would not recognize her and she could enter the inn without raising any suspicion. She walked past the dark alleyway in which she knew two of them were hiding, resisting the urge to look toward them. Even though she didn't look, the young Duende felt their eyes on her. She also felt a shiver run through her body, but she lifted her chin and kept walking. If she was right, that they knew nothing about her connection to Carling, they would not come after her. Fortunately, she was right.

Lilara entered the dimly lit main room of the inn to find Kelfy, Higson, Pik, Tibbals, and Tandum pacing back and forth, and peeking around the drawn curtains covering the windows.

"Lilara," squealed Tibbals once the door was shut. The Centaur rushed up to her and lowered herself to her equine knees. "We have been so worried about you and Carling. Did you see the Heilodius Centaurs? Did they see you? Is Carling alright?"

"One question at a time, filly," said Tandum, stepping up beside them. "Give her a chance to answer."

"Where is Carling?" said Higson, ignoring what Tandum had just said to his sister.

Lilara took a deep breath and let it out with a huff, trying to calm her jittery nerves. "Carling is fine. She is hiding in the old graveyard. I saw the Heilodius Centaurs. They have surrounded the building."

"How did ye get past 'em, little miss?" asked Pik.

"They weren't looking for me. I just walked right by," said Lilara with a smile on her face and a twinkle in her eye.

"What a clever girl ye be," the Faun said, patting her on the head.

Tibbals disappeared into a back room of the inn and returned with a cup of warm milk and a soft blanket to wrap around Lilara.

Tandum called the group together. "We need to get to the old graveyard. But Lilara says the Heilodius have surrounded the inn." Looking at Kelfy, he said, "Do you have any ideas?"

Kelfy stiffened. "Me? Why do you ask me?"

"Well, you live here," said Tandum, his facial expression and voice showing the effort it was taking for him to be patient with the Duende. "You know your way around. I thought, perhaps, you might have an idea about how we could escape."

"You want *me* to go out and face those monsters?" Kelfy said, his eyes narrowed.

"Certainly not if you don't want to," said Tandum with a sneer of disgust.

"Not if you're afraid to," added Higson with an equal dose of antipathy.

Kelfy crossed his arms with a snort and turned toward the fireplace. When he turned back around a few minutes later, he wore a new expression. A smile filled his face and his eyes were wide open. "I have a brilliant idea," he said. "Just leave it to me."

"What's your idea?" asked Tibbals.

"I'll climb out a back window, sneak past the Centaurs, and recruit some of our biggest and strongest Duende to send the Heilodius back where they came from."

"Do ye think the villagers will do that?" asked Pik.

"Sure, they will. You saw how they revered Carling when they found out she had the Silver Breastplate."

"Oh, Kelfy, what a wonderful idea," gushed Tibbals. "You are indeed a brave and true friend."

Kelfy turned to Higson, his mouth curved in a self-satisfied grin.

Higson narrowed his eyes and said nothing.

Kelfy grabbed a cloak and wrapped it tightly around his body. He pushed his hair back and covered his head with the cloak's hood. "I'll be back soon with help. When you hear a knock on the door, open it." With those parting words, he dashed into one of the side rooms and opened a ground-floor window just enough to squeezed through. He poked his hood-covered head out and looked both ways. Standing by the corner of the building were two Heilodius Centaurs, both wrapped in black capes that draped over their shivering haunches. Their tails hung limp with boredom. One was a hand taller than the other. The shorter one was pawing the ground with a front hoof. Kelfy glanced back over his shoulder. Certain no one was watching him, he crawled out the window.

Kelfy creeped up the narrow, cluttered alley toward the Centaurs. "Hey!" he shouted as he reached their hind legs and tails. "You there! You waiting for someone?"

The two Centaurs whirled around on their haunches. "Where'd you come from?" one of them asked, his eyes first open wide with surprise and then narrowed with suspicion.

"I was about to ask you the same thing. But I'll answer first. I live here. Now, what about you?"

"I don't see that's any o' yer business," said the Centaur named Reemer.

"Oh," Kelfy said, turning around and taking a few steps in the other direction. "Well then, I guess I can't help you then, can I?"

"Help us? Ha!" the first said with a snort. "And just what could you possibly do to help us?

Kelfy stopped and turned back around. "I guess that depends upon what you're doing."

"What does it look like we're doing, mister know-it-all?" said Reemer, swishing his tail and stomping a hoof.

"I think you're spying on the inn in hopes that the young Duende girl with the Silver Breastplate will appear."

The two Centaurs looked back and forth at one another as though trying to decide what to make of this and how to answer. Reemer shrugged his human-like shoulders. "Okay. You know what we're about. What does that have to do with you?"

"It has *everything* to do with me for I am the only one who *can* help you."

Reemer stomped his hoof and pressed his hands against his hips. "I'm getting tired of these riddles. Tell us why you're here or we'll throw you off a cliff right into the Swirling Sea!"

Kelfy held up his hand. "Easy there, big boy. You won't do that and we both know it. Without me, you will never get the girl you're seeking."

Reemer lowered his human torso and placed his face close to Kelfy's. Keeping his voice calm he said, "Tell us where she is."

Kelfy folded his arms across his chest and lifted his chin. "I will under one condition."

"Which is...?" both Centaurs said.

"I want out of this backward, repressive village. I'm sick of fish and the sea. I want to go with you, back to your leader, and have a leadership role when the Heilodius take over the throne."

The two centaurs reared up on their hind legs, pawing the air with their front hooves.

They dropped back down to the ground, their hooves striking showers of sparks across the flagstones.

"Such audacity!" said Reemer. "What makes you think Zarius would want *your* help running the kingdom?"

"I don't see that he has much choice if he wants to get the Silver Breastplate. But if you're not interested in accomplishing your assignment, I'll just be going." Kelfy swished his cape as he turned on his heels. He took one step.

"Wait!" commanded Reemer.

Kelfy smiled to himself. Dropping the smile and raising his eyebrows, he turned slowly around.

"What can you do to help us with our assignment?" the shorter Centaur demanded.

Kelfy lifted his chin. "I can deliver the girl. I know where she is and she isn't at the inn."

Quickly, a plan was hatched. "There are two young Centaurs, one short and stupid Duende lad, one little Duende girl, and one ugly Faun at the inn. All are unarmed as they lost their weapons on the way to the Isle of Hy-Basilia," said Kelfy, not knowing about the bow and quiver of arrows Carling had left in Pik's care. "How many of you are there?"

"Eight," said Reemer.

"Perfect. It shouldn't be hard for four or five of you to get control of the creatures at the inn. I'll take a few of you with me to the graveyard to gather up the girl."

It was agreed, and soon Kelfy was heading for the old graveyard with a few of the soldiers. The rest of the Heilodius Centaurs were rounded up and sent to the inn.

Unbeknownst to any of them, the entire interchange had been observed by Lilara from where she crouched behind a wooden barrel in the alleyway. She had silently followed Kelfy out the window. As soon as all parties left the vicinity of the inn to carry out their plan, Lilara ran toward the dock.

CHAPTER 35

Facing the Enemy with Integrity

CARLING SHIVERED IN THE cold night air and pressed herself closer to the jackal, absorbing some of his warmth. As tired as she was, she was unable to sleep. She continued to wonder what was keeping her friends. Why were they taking so long to come to the graveyard? The longer she sat in the cold, dark tomb, the more she worried. Clearly something was amiss. Lilara should not have taken this long to return with at least one of her friends.

She tried to calm her fears by stroking the jackal between his pointed, silver-tipped ears.

A branch cracked. Carling's hand, on its way to stroke the jackal's head again, froze in the air. A soft step echoed like a whisper. The jackal jerked his head up and the hackles on his back stood on end from his neck to the base of his tail. A low growl rumbled up from deep inside the wild animal.

Soon footfalls were heard crunching on the snow. The jackal rose only slightly until he was in a crouching position, his muscles tense, and growled again.

From the sound of the light two-beat footsteps, Carling was sure it wasn't a Centaur walking around in the graveyard. She crawled on her hands and knees toward the opening of the tomb; the jackal creeped along beside her, crouching low and still growling.

Carling peeked around the edge of the arched opening. As she did so, she heard Kelfy's voice in a loud whisper calling out to her.

"Carling...Carling...Carling, where are you?"

Relief and joy flooded through her. "Over here, Kelfy. I'm over here in the tomb."

She watched as Kelfy jogged through the snow, weaving around the tombstones. The jackal growled even louder and rocked back on his haunches, preparing to pounce.

Carling put her hand on the wild dog-like creature's head. "It's okay. He's a friend. You don't have to worry."

The jackal looked over at her, his eyes mere slits. Though still tense, he remained beside her.

When Kelfy reached the tomb and saw the jackal, he came to an abrupt halt and raised his hands with his palms out. "Is he friendly?" he asked Carling.

"He's my friend. He will not hurt you," said Carling, stroking the jackal's head. A soft, warning growl rolled through the jackal.

Kelfy hesitated, then cautiously stepped forward. When he reached Carling, he took her in his arms and hugged her tightly.

Tears trickled down Carling's cheeks. "Oh, I'm so glad you made it. I've been so worried." She pushed back and looked him in the eyes, trying to make out his expression in the darkness. "But where are the others? What has taken so long?"

"We must run and hide," Kelfy said, taking her hands in his, "for I tell you plainly we are in no small danger. We need to leave Madiera immediately!"

Carling narrowed her eyes and cocked her head. This didn't sound like Kelfy. It sounded too...she couldn't quite put her finger on her feelings. Perhaps it sounded too rehearsed. She felt the Stone of Integrity grow warm against her skin. "What do you mean? What has happened?" she said, her voice quivering.

"The Heilodius have taken all the others captive. Without weapons, they had no chance. Only I was able to escape."

Carling gasped and her hand flew to her mouth as her eyes flew open. Rehearsed or not, what he was saying filled her with a sense of panic. "We must go help them," she shouted.

"We can't," Kelfy said. "We would be greatly outnumbered. We wouldn't have a chance."

"If you were not my friend, I'd say those are the words of a coward," said Carling, her body tense with anger. She crossed her arms over her chest, feeling the warmth of the Silver Breastplate.

"I am only concerned about keeping you safe, my beautiful Carling," Kelfy said, cradling Carling's chin in his hands. He gazed through the darkness into her violet eyes. "I have no concern for my own well-being."

The jackal growled and walked around them, keeping his eyes, now glinting red, on Kelfy.

Carling's head was spinning as she struggled to make sense of what she was hearing and feeling. This did not seem like the Kelfy she had come to know and even love. The Stone of Integrity, burning against her chest, was telling her that something was terribly wrong.

The winter wind was picking up as the dawn approached. She heard the naked branches of the willows that lined the graveyard as they rattled against one another. Tiny flakes of snow began falling sideways outside the tomb. Her thoughts were as confused as the blowing snowflakes. *Which direction should I go?* she asked herself. Yet, she knew there was only one acceptable answer. The Stones of Light, set in the Silver Breastplate, were warm, telling her what to do. "I will not leave without my friends. We must go back and help them," she said. She lifted her chin and set her jaw to end the discussion.

Kelfy stepped back, nodding. "I feared you would give that answer. If that is your decision, then I will go with you. We will face the enemy together."

Kelfy took her hand and pulled Carling forward. Just as they stepped out of the tomb and into the falling snow, Heilodius Centaurs leaped out from behind various tombstones. With swords drawn, they surrounded them.

Carling gasped and clutched Kelfy who abruptly pushed her away. "I'm sorry, Your Majesty," he said with a sneer as he moved away from her and stepped up beside one of the Centaurs. "I have new allegiances now."

Carling felt her heart fall to her stomach. "W-what is the meaning of this, Kelfy?" she stammered.

"You're my ticket out of this horrible place," Kelfy said. "One thing I've learned as a fisherman is to go the way the wind blows, and right now it's blowing toward the Heilodius Herd. I'm sure you can understand that I must look out for myself. I have dreams, too, you know."

Even in the dim light of dawn, Carling could see the betrayal in his eyes...eyes which had appeared so warm and loving just a few moments ago, were now cold and dark. Her mouth fell open and she slowly shook her head. "I thought you were my friend," she whispered.

"Why so shocked?" he asked. "You're the one with the Stone of Integrity, not me."

Carling had no more words to say. She just looked down at her feet, ice cold in the snow, and shivered.

Just then the jackal leaped out of the tomb toward one of the Centaurs, growling and howling. The Centaur spun around and let both back legs fly, catching the jackal in the chest. With a yelp, the jackal dropped to the ground, his blood staining the snow.

"No!" cried Carling as she dashed to the side of the jackal and dropped to her knees beside it. The jackal's eyes closed and his breathing stopped. Carling looked up and glared at the Centaur. "You killed him!"

"He was just a worthless animal," said the soldier with a snort and a swish of his tail. "Besides, he attacked me first."

"Let's go," said Reemer, their leader. "The others will meet us on the edge of town."

The power of the Silver Breastplate had been noised about among the Heilodius Centaurs, especially by those who had witnessed the death of Clank more than a year before. It was not something any of them were likely to forget. As a result, they seemed afraid to touch Carling. Instead, they stood back and shouted their commands at her.

"Get moving," said one of the Heilodius Centaurs in a loud, harsh voice.

"If you want to see your friends alive, you'll do as we say," said another in an equally unpleasant tone.

Carling slowly arose. With the elegance of a queen, she lifted her chin and turned to leave the graveyard. Just as they reached the rusted, twisted, iron fence of the graveyard, an ear-piercing meow filled the air. At the same instant, Hilgalda's cat leaped out of the shadows and onto the back of one of the Centaurs. She dug her claws into the equine back and sank her sharp fangs into the Centaur's human shoulder. With a cry of pain, the Centaur began bucking and rearing, trying desperately to dislodge the beast. Unsuccessful, he dropped to the ground, intent on crushing the cat beneath his weight, his sword falling from his hand as he did so.

Carling dashed forward, grabbed the sword and pivoted to face the others as the cat snarled and hung on to the Centaur, which continued to thrash around on the ground. She saw a look of fear pass across Kelfy's face as he backed up and tried to hide behind a crumbling tombstone.

Reemer narrowed his eyes and lifted his sword over his head. With a shout, he charged toward Carling, snow flying from his hooves. Carling spun around. With a crash, the two swords met, sending sparks through the air. Carling finished her swing, her momentum sending her around in a circle. She ducked, narrowly avoiding being struck by a second swing from Reemer's sword. She stepped to one side to get her bearings just as another Centaur advanced. She blocked his sword but stumbled backward, tripping over a broken branch concealed beneath the snow. She landed on her back with a *"humph."* While the one Centaur continued to fight off the cat, the other three stepped up and surrounded her.

"Get up!" ordered Reemer.

Carling rolled over and pushed herself up to her feet. She turned her head and gasped. The cat lay on the snow, not moving, and the Centaur the cat had so bravely attacked was scrambling to his feet. "I'll take my sword, thank you," he said to Carling. She dropped it. Its sharp point pierced the frozen ground. He reached down and jerked it loose.

Carling looked back to where the cat had been lying in the snow just a moment before and blinked her eyes in surprise. The cat was gone.

Kelfy returned from his hiding spot to lead the way through the iron gate that marked the entrance to the graveyard. Surrounded by the Heilodius Centaurs with swords drawn, Carling, her head high, her eyes as hard as steel and staring straight ahead, marched through the snow behind him. A tear rolled down her cheek. She lifted her hand and brushed it away. Carling was feeling very alone and very frightened. Her thoughts went to the Wizard. *Where is he?* she wondered.

Kelfy took them to the edge of town. There they found the rest of the Heilodius Centaurs, swords drawn and pointed at Tibbals, Tandum, Higson, and Pik. Lilara was nowhere to be seen. Deep gashes, still dripping blood, covered the chests and flanks of the Heilodius, sure signs that Tibbals and Tandum had used their powerful back hooves to fight them off. But it was not enough, for Tibbals and Tandum now stood, heads bowed, in the center of the ring of soldiers. Tibbals's long, blond hair was a nest of tangles and her lovely blouse was torn to shreds. Tandum didn't look much better, and Pik was equally ruffled.

Higson, only partially recovered from his ordeal in Hilgalda's laboratory, was sitting on Tandum's back, still looking groggy. As soon as he saw Carling approaching, surrounded by Heilodius Centaurs, he slid off the Centaur's back and stumbled toward her. His path was immediately blocked by crossed swords.

"Not so fast, little guy," snarled one of the soldiers. "You're not going anywhere."

Higson shook his fist at the soldier. "Let me go to Carling."

"Not a chance. Now step back or we'll have Duende kabobs for dinner." This made the other Heilodius laugh.

Higson pursed his lips and glared at them all.

It was Tibbals who noticed that Kelfy was leading them, and not as a prisoner. "Kelfy!" she exclaimed. "What are you doing?"

A dark shadow passed over Kelfy's face and he scowled at Tibbals. One of the Heilodius beside him patted him on the shoulder and said, "He's one of us, now."

"One of you?" Tibbals responded. "Impossible! I don't believe it."

"Not so impossible," sneered Higson, his voice slurring the words. "I never trusted him."

"You're just jealous because she liked me more than you," said Kelfy with a snort, prompting Carling to glare at him.

"But you've betrayed us," said Tandum, the veins over his temple pulsing in anger. "You've betrayed Carling."

Kelfy narrowed his eyes and said, "I sensed the scales tilting in the direction of Zarius and his band. I wasn't born a prince like you, Tandum. If I'm ever to get out of Madiera, I have to make it happen myself."

"Enough of this banter," said one of the Heilodius Centaurs. "We have a long way to go."

"You're not going anywhere!"

All heads turned toward the sound. A tiny Duende stepped out from behind a tree. Lilara.

"Oh?" said one soldier as he pawed the ground with a front hoof. "And what is a little pipsqueak like you going to do to stop us?"

Just as he said that, Hilgalda the Witch appeared on the top of a boulder. Her yellow cat stepped up beside her, twitching her tail and curling her lips to reveal her fangs which were stained with Centaur blood. "She isn't alone," said the witch, thrusting her fist in the air.

From around every tree stepped a Duende. Pitchforks, shovels, bows and arrows and even a few swords were held high in the villagers' hands. "She has all of us to help," shouted one of the Duende, whom Carling recognized as a fisherman from the dock. All the Duende shook their makeshift weapons in agreement. "We won't let you harm our queen!"

With a shout, the Duende charged. The Heilodius Centaurs were so shocked, they just stood in place, their heads and tails up, their mouths open. But when the first blows were struck, they started fighting back.

Lilara tossed swords to Tibbals and Tandum.

The conflict began with flashing swords and flying hooves. The Duende had the advantage of being able to dash around between the Centaurs' legs, leaving them spinning around in circles most of the time. While the Centaurs had the advantage of skill with a sword, these skills did little good when long pitchforks and shovels were stabbing them in their hocks, haunches, backs, and barrels.

While Tibbals, Tandum, Pik, and the Duende from Madiera kept the Centaurs both confused and busy, Carling ran and Higson stumbled toward Kelfy. Reaching him at the same time, they tackled him, the force of their impact smashing Kelfy to the ground. He immediately began swinging his arms, kicking his legs, and rolling from side to side. Carling grabbed his arms and held on even though she was getting pulled back and forth. Higson, his teeth clenched and eyes narrowed in hatred, began punching the traitor in the face.

"Higson, stop. Just grab his legs," said Carling.

"I won't stop," shouted Higson, throwing another blow and getting a kick in the stomach in return.

"I've got him. Stop hitting him. You're hurting him!"

"I intend to hurt him," Higson growled as he grabbed Kelfy's neck with both hands. "He's a traitor. He turned you...all of us...over to the Heilodius."

As Kelfy began to gag, Carling said, "Higson, I command you to stop!"

Because of the power and authority in Carling's voice, Higson's eyes opened wide. He inhaled deeply and let go of Kelfy's neck. "Why?" he asked, brushing his hair back from his face and staring at Carling. "He's a traitor," he repeated, spitting in Kelfy's face. "He should pay for what he's done."

"Even a traitor may mend," said Carling, more quietly. She looked down at Kelfy, her eyes filled with sorrow. She looked back at Higson. "But he can't mend if he's dead. We will see that he pays for his crimes without committing new ones ourselves."

Lilara appeared at their side, holding a fishing net. "Here," she said. "Wrap him up in this."

CHAPTER 36

Not the End

WHEN THE WINTER WIND swept the snow clouds further inland, the remnants of the battle were left behind. The crushed snow was stained with blood. The villagers were moaning in pain from their injuries. Tibbals, Tandum, and Pik stood silently, watching the retreating Heilodius Centaurs disappear over the hills that bordered Madiera. The victory was not something to celebrate, merely something to be grateful for.

Carling stood silently, watching Kelfy being led away by the village constable. When he was out of sight, she sucked in her breath, squared her shoulders, and turned her attention to the injured Duende scattered around on the snow.

The Duende from the village of Madiera had fought hard and suffered much, all to protect their queen. They were fishermen, not soldiers, and their inexperience in battle had resulted in many being injured. But their devotion to their future queen made up for any ineptitude they'd displayed as warriors.

The thought of their loyalty brought tears to Carling's eyes. She hurried from one injured Duende to another, attempting to help where she could. Carling whispered words of appreciation to each. "Thank you for rescuing me," she said to one. "Thank you for coming to my aid," she said to another. Moving further, she came upon a Duende lying in the snow beneath a tree. She gasped when she realized it was the innkeeper. Unable to suppress her surprise at finding him there among the injured she said, "*You* came to help me? Why?"

"I do not doubt that every one of us would risk our lives willingly to save the life of our dear queen," he said in a weak, trembling voice.

Tandum stepped up beside them. Overhearing the innkeeper's reply, he said. "Easy to say, now that we've won. Last stands make good stories to tell our grandchildren around the hearth on cold winter nights."

"Well," the innkeeper said, "I hope to tell this story by my warm hearth tonight and for many years of cold nights to come." He forced a smile before being overcome with a coughing fit.

"I wonder what your story would be had we lost and you lived to tell it," said Tandum.

The innkeeper coughed and grabbed his stomach. He looked up at Tandum and Carling. "I understand your suspicions, my friend. I deserve them."

Tandum stared down at the old Duende as though considering what he should do, what he should believe. He smiled briefly and let out a sigh.

"I trust that your motives were pure, my friend," Tandum said as he scooped up the innkeeper. "I will carry you to your hearth."

As Tandum helped the injured innkeeper, Carling turned to see who else might need assistance. She noticed Pernilla Persdotter and other women from the village taking care of the few remaining wounded. Suddenly exhausted and with the shock of Kelfy's betrayal still weighing heavily on her heart Carling headed back to the inn, clutching Higson's arm. She walked silently, allowing the tears that were stinging the backs of her eyes to flow freely down her cheeks and mingle with the snowflakes. Losing someone one thought was a friend is very painful, even for a queen.

As she approached the inn, she noticed the looming clouds in the sky had become lower and darker, matching her mood. The wind whirled between the little shops and houses, sending the snow into deep drifts against the sides of the buildings. It was a bleak day and Carling wished she had her mother beside her to help her. *But I must face this alone,* she thought, her tears flowing down her cheeks again.

Lilara was already at the inn, fixing a much-needed meal. No one spoke as they, even Tibbals, ate the fish stew, each lost in their own thoughts.

As for Carling, she couldn't get thoughts of Kelfy and his betrayal out of her mind. She had trusted Kelfy completely and had not, even for a moment, thought he would ever turn on her for his own glory.

How did he manage to fool me? Was my attraction to him the cause of my blindness? And Higson. What of him? It was obvious that he never liked Kelfy. Yet, I thought he was just being childish. I pushed aside his comments as signs of trivial, boyish jealousy or, perhaps, bothersome over-protectiveness. I need to face the fact that Higson was right all along. Perhaps, she told herself, *I need to pay closer attention to what he says from now on...if there is a now on.*

Carling looked over at Higson and her heart ached. He was scowling as he ate his stew, not looking at or talking to anyone. For the first time, she saw the hurt she had caused him. She resolved, then and there, that she would make it up to her best friend. Somehow, she would show him how much he meant to her...had always meant to her.

After dinner, everyone scattered to their rooms. All were exhausted, having foregone sleep for two days in addition to enduring a difficult battle. Tibbals gave Carling a hug before the Centaur entered her room. Higson passed by her without saying a word.

"Higson...Higson, please stop."

Higson stopped in the hallway, his back to her.

"I'm sorry I hurt you. I promise I'll make it up to you," Carling said. "You were right about Kelfy. I see that now."

Higson slowly turned back to face her. The grim line of his mouth relaxed and his eyes softened. "We'll talk later," he said. He turned away and went into his room without saying anything else.

Carling bit her lip and struggled to keep more tears from escaping her eyes. She sighed and opened the door to her room.

The little queen was surprised to see the oil lamp by her bed glowing brightly. But even more surprising was the visitor who had seemingly lit the lamp.

Shim, the Tommy Knocker, the guardian of the Stone of Courage, looked up at her from where he sat cross-legged on her bed. He uncrossed his short legs and extended his large feet which were protected by heavy boots with curled-up toes. He pushed his tiny body to the floor. His large, round, blue eyes twinkled beneath his bushy eyebrows...eyebrows that were bouncing up and down. "Surprised to see me?" he said, rubbing his whiskered face and managing a smile.

"Actually...yes," Carling said. She was equally surprised that she felt the tiniest bit *happy* to see him.

Shim giggled. "I thought you would be."

Shim shuffled forward, holding his cane in one hand. His other hand was outstretched toward the red Stone of Courage, trembling slightly. "My beloved...," he whispered. He stopped just before reaching Carling and jerked his hand back. "Yes. Such a pity. Such a pity. Ah but such is life. It comes and it goes."

Carling interrupted his rambling. "Why have you come, Shim?"

Shim shook his head and blinked his eyes, bringing his thoughts back to the present. "Oh yes...why have I come? Well, to protect my beloved stone, of course. You seem to have quite the talent for putting it in danger."

"True that," mumbled Carling as she looked down at the Silver Breastplate with its three sparkling jewels.

"I have come to warn you," Shim said, dancing around her as nimble as a cat while twirling his crooked cane in the air.

"Warn me about what?" Carling said, not quite sure she wanted to hear. She tried to keep her eyes on the Tommy Knocker as he flitted about the room.

"The Heilodius Centaurs you defeated today were just a few of the many Zarius has sent to find you," Shim said as he pulled himself back up on the bed and resumed his cross-legged position.

"I'm not surprised. He doesn't like me very much."

"No, he doesn't. But that's Centaurs for you. Too bad they aren't more horse and less human. Then they wouldn't have such bad tempers and carry such heavy grudges."

Carling couldn't suppress a chuckle.

"In any case, he is a bad enemy to have. You seem to be collecting a lot of enemies."

"I have also made some wonderful friends," she said, thinking of the loyalty displayed by the Fairies and the fishermen...and even Hilgalda and her cat.

Shim raised his bushy eyebrows and scratched the bridge of his large nose. "Perhaps that's true...it remains to be seen. But I suppose that is neither here nor there. At the moment, my concern is for my beloved stone. So, I have come to warn you to leave this smelly village immediately. Once word reaches Zarius that you are here, he will destroy the village in order to find you. If you want to protect these poor, pitiful fishermen, you must leave." Shim hopped off the bed and bounced from one foot to the other. "Mark my warning. Do not stay another day in Madiera."

And then he was gone and Carling was alone with the silence he left behind, and her fears for the many who stood beside her, only to be put in danger again and again.

To be continued...

The Centaur Chronicles
Book 4
The Stone of Wisdom

The fable about the king and the seeds in Chapter 5 is from an ancient Mandarin Chinese story. It is a story I remember from my childhood, and I have retold it here in my own words and to the best of my recollection. M.J.E.

ABOUT THE

AUTHOR

Award-winning author, M.J. Evans loves her Savior, her family, her friends, her horses and poodle, and writing...in that order. A life-long equestrian, she enjoys competing in dressage and exploring the mountain trails on horseback.

Oh, and one more thing: she loves getting letters from her readers, too!

Find her email address on her website:

Dancinghorsepress.com

Read more books by M.J. Evans

The Mist Trilogy:
Behind the Mist
Mists of Darkness
The Rising Mist
Winner of the Gold Medal from the Mom's Choice Awards

North Mystic
First Place winner of the Purple Dragonfly Award

In the Heart of a Mustang
Gold medal winner from the Literary Classics Awards
Silver Medal winner from the Nautilus Awards
Silver Medal winner from the Readers' Favorite Awards
Equus Film Festival Winnie Award

The Centaur Chronicles:
Book 1 – The Stone of Mercy
Gold medal winner from the Feathered Quill Awards
Silver Medal winner from the Literary Classics Awards
Equus Film Festival Winnie Award
Book 2 – The Stone of Courage
Book Excellence Award
5 Star Award from the Readers' Favorite Reviews
Coming soon:
Book 4 – The Stone of Wisdom

Follow her blog: themisttrilogy.blogspot.com

Follow her on Instagram: mjevansbooks

"Like" her pages on Facebook:
Behind the Mist
North Mystic
In the Heart of a Mustang